BARRACK FOUR

ELYSE HOFFMAN

ISBN 978-1-952742-01-9 (ebook)

Project 613 Publishing
Project613Publishing.com

PROJECT613

CONTENTS

Barrack Four   7

Afterword   101

Dedicated to my mother and father for their enduring support
To my grandfather whose stories I never heard
To the children who suffered during the Holocaust
And to God, Who makes all stories

BARRACK FOUR

"So then my dad shot it!"

"No way!"

"It's true! Right in the head! Knocked it out!"

"Was it a big snake?"

"Mm hm..."

"How the hell'd he hit it on the head?"

"Dad was a great shot!"

"I don't believe you!"

"Vilém, Vilém, back me up here!"

Vilém Rehor, who was midway through his third beer of the night, barely heard his friend over the hubbub of the bar. He, his best friend Erik, and a pretty girl that his friend had been trying to put the moves on for the last half-hour were clustered around the counter. Erik was standing close to the girl, leaning on the table, while she sat beside the slightly slumped-over Vilém.

Vilém was far too exhausted to try and score himself. He had been hoping for a nice night out with his buddy, a few beers and some jokes, but Erik had never been one to pass up a conversation with a lovely lady.

He finished his drink, exhaled, and glanced over at his two companions. The bar was so dark that he could hardly see either the girl or his friend, but he could make out Erik's features enough to see him mouth three words: *help me out.*

Normally, he wouldn't. Their tradition was that Erik would make up some story off the top of his head and Vilém would teasingly decry it as either false or exaggerated. The girls never cared: it was a story, and as long as the story was good, they normally didn't mind if it was one hundred percent true or not.

But this time he was just so damn *tired* that he didn't feel like doing his usual routine. Besides, for once Erik had told a story that was above seventy-five percent true —his father *had* shot a snake with a BB gun once, Erik had just exaggerated his own bravery. From what Vilém remembered, Erik had been cowering in his tree house for hours on end, sobbing even after he was told the snake was gone.

"All true," Vilém assured the girl, gesturing to himself. "Witness."

"Wooow!" she cooed, finally giving him her full attention. "So you two have been friends for a real long time?"

"Since we were kids," said Erik, looking worriedly over at Vilém and quirking his head to the side, obviously finding the fact that Vilém wasn't taking part in their usual repartee disturbing.

"Hey, buddy, you okay?" he asked. "You're looking a little, eh…"

"Dead?" Vilém supplied, rolling his aching shoulders and smirking. Erik and the girl both snickered.

"Yeah," agreed Erik.

"Too much to drink?" the girl queried, snatching Vilém's empty glass and putting it upside-down on the counter. He shook his head.

"Nah ah, I was just up all day," he explained.

"Ya' mean all night?" asked the girl.

"Nope, night-shifter," replied Vilém, smiling at her playful theft of his cup. He tried to steal it back, but she moved it before he could. He chuckled and decided to wait until she let her guard down.

"Ooh," she said with an understanding nod. "What are you, security?"

"Yep, good guess!"

"Yay, I'm smart!" the girl giggled. "Where?"

Vilém and Erik exchanged awkward glances. They had made a list long ago of "Topics To Avoid While Trying To Score." While they had never officially added "The Holocaust" to that list, ever since Vilém had gotten a job at the local concentration camp it had become that list's unspoken #1. There was no better way to spoil the mood than to bring up the most infamous genocide in world history, after all.

But since Vilém was fairly sure that Erik had already charmed this girl, he decided there would be no harm in being honest tonight.

"You know that concentration camp right outside town?" he asked. The girl's eyes—which Vilém had just noticed were a lovely shade of chestnut brown —widened.

"*There?*" she gasped. Erik cringed at her horrified tone, shaking his head at Vilém, silently chastising him for bringing up the #1.

"He guards that shitty place during the night, I fix up clogged sinks during the day," Erik joked, trying to add a hint of humor to the dark subject. "I'm boring, he's depressing."

"Oh, yes," concurred Vilém. "I'm depressing."

"You don't seem *that* depressing," the girl noted with a brightness in her tone that made Vilém raise a surprised eyebrow.

"Man, I'd never be able to work there," she sighed, fiddling with Vilém's empty cup and gazing at her distorted reflection in the glass. "Too…"

"Depressing?" queried Vilém.

"Yeah, yeah. And it's kind of worse for me cause I'm Jewish, so it'd be like…wow, that could have been me! You know? I've never even been able to visit that place. My family's been avoiding it for basically three generations."

"Totally understand," he said.

"You're Jewish?" queried Erik with a smile. "Hey, cool! Half Jewish right here!"

"Mazel tov!" she declared. She looked over at Vilém, nodding her head as though to question his Jewishness (or lack thereof.)

"Grandpa on my mom's side," Vilém said. "You should have heard the argument he and my pa had when my folks decided not to get me circumcised."

She laughed and Erik, sensing the chemistry

brewing between the two (a chemistry based on a bleak history, but any chemistry that didn't blow up in Vilém's face was good chemistry), decided to search elsewhere. He spotted a pretty brunette sitting by herself and pretended she was an old classmate of his.

"Have fun, Vilém! Don't be a moron!" he cried as he sauntered over to the other girl.

"Look who's talking!" Vilém retorted. The chestnut-eyed girl giggled and scooted closer, finally allowing Vilém to get a good look at her as the light illuminated her face and body. She was most certainly pretty. Maybe a little chubbier than the cultural ideal, but she had a nice body, a beautiful face, and the cutest dimples he'd ever seen.

"Oh, I'm Vilém, by the way," he said, offering his hand. She gave it a firm, genial shake.

"Jana, in case you missed it," she said. "Sorry. I guess I was giving Erik all my attention. You barely got a glance at my ugly face!"

"Nooo!" he said, shaking his head. "I'm the only ugly one here! I know I look like crap. I got *no* sleep."

"Why not?"

"Well, I was *gonna* sleep during the day like I usually do and hang with Erik tonight, but I had stuff I wanted to get done and by the time Erik came to pick me up I was just…"

He pretended to fall over dead. Jana snickered and he took advantage of her distraction to reclaim his cup.

"Heeey, cheater!" she cried as he hugged his glass protectively.

"We weren't *officially* having a competition. Besides, I'm not drunk *yet*," he said.

"So, what were you doing that robbed you of your beauty sleep?" Jana inquired.

"Writing!" he declared with a hint of pride. Her eyes brightened.

"Oh, you're an author?"

"Well, not yet. I'm practicing. It takes a million words of crap before you write something decent."

"What're you writing about?" Jana asked. Vilém glanced idly at the ceiling.

Since he didn't want her to think he was *completely* insane, he decided not to tell her about Raya Pomnenka, the ghost of the Holocaust victim he had promised to always remember. He was writing her story as insurance for that vow. Even if someday he wasn't around to remember her, a book or short story could memorialize her for eternity. He had failed to get a plaque dedicated to her installed in the Camp. To get permission to erect such a memorial, he would have to prove her existence, and there was nothing material left of her. A book, even if people thought it was fiction, would have to do. It was better than nothing.

But telling Jana all that likely wouldn't be the best way to get her number.

"Something I thought of at work. Maybe I'll show you when I'm done," he said.

"Cool!"

"I'll warn you: it'll be depressing. Holocaust and all that."

"I don't mind. I grew up reading about it, I just wouldn't be able to be *there* constantly. Why'd you take that job?"

"Well, to be honest I mostly took it 'cause of the paycheck. Times are tough."

"Right, right."

"And I *hated* it at first, it completely creeped me out. But y'know, I'm actually really glad I took it. It's been... an experience. It's depressing, but I feel like it's important."

"Oh, yeah. And hey, it gave you inspiration!"

"Right!"

"Do you have to do a lot at night? Like, do people stick around after dark?"

"Not...willingly," Vilém said, remembering the shy, gentle presence of Raya Pomnenka. "But when they do, I help them out. That's my job."

Jana nodded, smiling softly.

"You seem like a really nice guy," she observed.

"And you," he declared, waving towards the bartender, "are a really nice and really pretty girl. So... let me buy you a drink and let's talk about you. Are you as depressing as I am?"

"Not really," Jana said, smiling at the bartender as he filled Vilém's cup and plopped a beer in front of her.

"Then let's talk about happy things," Vilém suggested.

"Rainbows and butterflies for the rest of the night?" Jana joked.

"Rainbows and butterflies," he agreed, raising his glass. She clinked her cup against his.

"Cheers!" she declared, and the rest of their stay at the bar consisted of drinking, laughing, joking, and sharing stories that were anything but depressing before they ended up stumbling out of the building together.

13

Vilém would never describe himself as a player. He'd had his fair share of one-night stands, but he'd never been the sort to skedaddle the second he awoke, leaving the poor girl potentially confused and hurt. Even if it was a girl he found significantly less lovely come morning when the beer goggles dissipated, he always stayed until she showed him a smile.

He didn't need to force himself to stick around for Jana's sake: she was just as pretty in the morning as she had been when his brain had been addled with alcohol. His tradition of staying ended up serving him well. They had gone back to her apartment, and not only was her kitchen fully stocked, but she knew how to make chocolate-chip pancakes.

"Haven't had these since I was...ten? Probably ten," Vilém declared with a boyish smile after getting dressed and sitting down at the table. Jana chuckled.

"What? Shame! I'll just have to spoil you."

"You're already spoiling me!" he cried as she served him a sumptuous mountain of pancakes.

"Aw, you deserve it. You're a sweetheart," she said, pulling her hair out of a ponytail and letting it fall over her shoulders. "Thanks for not jumping outta my window when I wasn't looking. I can sometimes get pretty dumb at the bar. I've taken some real bastards home...nothing too bad, but y'know, sometimes sweethearts turn sour in the morning. You're great, though... in more ways than one."

She smiled coyly and he felt his face heat up.

"Er...thanks..." he mumbled, practically hiding behind his tower of pancakes so she wouldn't see how red he was.

"Eat up!" giggled Jana. He grinned.

"Happily!" he declared, taking a bite.

"Well?" she asked.

"Great! Really sweet!" he proclaimed, and Jana's face lit up with joy.

"I'm glad," she said. "I'd have to quit my job otherwise!"

"What's your job?"

"You know that candy store on Klammer Street?"

"Sladký Sweets? Mm hm! Love that place! Too bad I didn't spend my whole childhood here, I would'a spent my whole allowance there!"

"Haha! You would'a given *me* your allowance if you had! It's my shop!"

"You *own* the place?"

"Family business. Since my dad ran off with some Hungarian girl and my big brother's off in Berlin studying, I'm in charge. My grandma lives right above the shop. She still helps run it, but she signed the shop over to me. Said I have the most passion for the place."

"Is she all right on her own?"

Jana snorted.

"What?"

"Nothing," said Jana, sipping her coffee, a smirk peeking out over the rim of the mug. "It's just that if you knew my grandma, you wouldn't say that. She could kick your butt."

"Really?"

"Yep!"

"I *am* a security guard."

"She could do it."

"All right, I'll take your word for it. So what's it like, running a candy shop?"

"Both wonderful and awful."

"Awful? I work at a concentration camp—you're gonna have to try *hard* to convince me that working at a candy shop is awful!"

"Oh, I love it, and I imagine it's a more...*cheerful* environment than what you have to deal with. It's just I love it too much—I'm *so* freaking fat because of that place."

"Oh, come on, you're beautiful!"

"And you're a liar...but a real sweet one."

"I'm not a liar. Actually, the only one that's gonna end up fat around here is me. I'm gonna be coming over to your house for breakfast every day now!"

"Haha! Won't even bother with the pleasantries, you're just gonna climb through my window every morning," she giggled.

"That's the plan, I'm part of your morning routine now," Vilém said.

"Sounds good to me!" Jana said, quickly tidying her countertop. "I've got to run to work. You gonna steal everything I own?"

"Nope!"

"Then stay as long as you want and finish up."

"You're an angel!"

"You deserve it. Did you give me your number last night?"

"Let me check...nope!"

They exchanged numbers, an embrace, and a

promise to meet up again before Jana ran upstairs, did her makeup, and hurried to work. Vilém looked down at the new contact on his phone with glee before noticing a missed call from Erik. He inhaled deeply and called his friend.

"Before you even ask, yes, yes we did," he said as soon as his friend picked up. Erik chuckled.

"Good one, Vil! She was hot! Where are ya' now?"

"Her house. She made breakfast and let me stay for a little while. Real sweet girl."

"Oooh, do I sense domestic bliss already settling in?"

"Shut up. Speaking of sweet, did you know she owns that little candy shop?"

"Sladký's?"

"Yup!"

"Oh, yeah, awesome place! They have great fudge."

"I think she might be a keeper."

"Because of the candy?"

"Erik…"

"I'm kidding. Hey, Vil, if she's a nice girl, go for it. Just because your job's depressing doesn't mean your life has to be depressing too."

"Guess you're right. Hey, listen, bud, I'm gonna finish up here and clean up, maybe hang out at home before I run to work. I'll meet up with ya' when I can."

"Sounds cool! Gotta head to work myself. Not all of us are night owls like you!"

"See ya, bud!"

"Good luck at work, Vil. Don't let that place get to you!"

"I'll try."

ALTHOUGH HE HAD GROWN MORBIDLY accustomed to the Camp, it was hard to obey Erik's command and not let the place get to him. Even when he was in the best mood he'd had in a while, the second the bus screeched to a halt and he saw the tall, warped barbed-wire fence, his smile wilted like a neglected rosebush.

"Another night," he sighed, adjusting his uniform and skittering off the bus, carefully pushing his way through a small cluster of college students. He grunted when he saw two girls pose as one lifted up a selfie stick and snapped a picture of her and her friend in front of the Camp. At least they weren't smiling. Nevertheless, he felt the need to speak up.

"Girls, *please*," he sighed. "Show some respect."

One girl blushed in embarrassment. The other huffed.

"We're just getting a picture. Everyone's doing it," she said, pointing towards another student, who was taking a picture of one of the wooden watchtowers.

"They're taking pictures of the Camp for school. You're treating it like a vacation," Vilém pointed out. "People died here. A lot of them. Try to keep the focus on them instead of you."

The huffy girl's scowl melted away and she gave a small, resigned nod.

"'Kay, sorry," she said, gesturing for her girlfriend to follow her back to the bus.

"Thanks for that, Rehor," a familiar female voice grunted. Vilém inhaled deeply and turned to face his boss, Ms. Doubek. Alica Doubek was a senior with curly silver hair and a perpetual scowl; it seemed as though she was constantly annoyed with all Creation. She always dressed in a suit (he had never seen her wear a dress and the day she wore one was likely the day Hell froze over) with a blood-red tie. A pair of reading glasses hung from her collar, reading glasses she never seemed inclined to put on: she always insisted on leaning horribly close to anything she felt like reading rather than don her spectacles.

Erik had once described Ms. Doubek as having a six-foot pole permanently stuck up her ass, and Vilém couldn't disagree. Compliments were a rare gift from the woman, and a smile...well, he didn't even know what it would look like if she were to smile. Some of the other employees at the Camp even referred to her as "The Kommandant" behind her back. Vilém never went that far.

"Ma'am?" he queried, and she pointed stiffly towards the retreating girls.

"Those girls," she said with a tut. "If one more idiot teen takes out one of those phone sticks, I'm going to grab it out of their greasy little mitts and beat them with it."

Vilém could easily visualize that, and the fact that he could do so without difficulty scared him.

"Disrespectful. My..." Her voice trailed off. "Well, never mind. Good work there, Rehor."

"No problem, ma'am. I agree; it is disrespectful," said Vilém, smiling slightly. Ever since the Raya Pomnenka graffiti incident, his relationship with his boss had been rather sour. He knew he was constantly walking on a tightrope with her. She hadn't forgiven him for failing to capture the vandal. Even though the girl had stopped carving her name onto the wall, the damage had been done to both Barrack Five and Vilém's reputation. Any amount of praise from his boss was a step towards forgiveness and was, to Vilém, almost as precious as his paycheck.

"Camp's closing up. You have your flashlight, Rehor?" asked Doubek. Vilém nodded, holding up the hefty tool.

"Good. I want you to stay near the Heydrich Exhibit for the next three weeks."

That made Vilém raise an eyebrow. "Heydrich Exhibit?" he repeated. Doubek beckoned for him to follow her. He obeyed, trailing behind his boss like a lost puppy as she strutted past Barrack Five and into Barrack Four.

A few straggling visitors were snapping pictures of the red and black placards and glass cases that were strategically spread out across the barrack. A new mini exhibit had been set up, probably last night while Vilém had been off. The placards prominently featured pictures of the Nazi official that had been in charge of Czechoslovakia during the war, the "Butcher of Prague", Reinhard Heydrich.

"It's actually supposed to be an exhibit about perpetrators," explained Doubek. "But we couldn't find much about the Kommandant except basic biographical information, and that's not enough to interest most people. So Heydrich gets to take center-stage this time."

"Yay for him," grumbled Vilém, leaning over one of

the glass cases and gazing at a small, slightly rusted pen that had evidently belonged to the Butcher.

"Don't touch!" snapped Doubek as Vilém's hand brushed against the glass. "That's the sort of behavior I need you to keep under control. Half of this stuff is on loan from other museums and the other half was from the bastard's family. I do *not* want to be getting a call from his son at six-in-the-morning asking why we destroyed his daddy's favorite pen. Until the folks in charge give us permission to take down the exhibit and send all this shit back, this room is your number one priority. Got it?"

"Yes, ma'am," said Vilém with an obedient nod.

"Good. Then stay here until closing. And if we have another Graffiti Girl incident, Rehor, you're fired."

"Y-yes, ma'am," said Vilém, bowing his head. She peered at him for a few seconds before giving a curt nod and marching out of the barrack. Vilém sighed and leaned against a placard without looking.

Once he'd recovered from his boss' threat, he glanced idly to the side and cringed when he discovered he was leaning right beside a picture of Heydrich. The Nazi's narrow eyes seemed to glare straight at him, as if Heydrich's ghost was possessing the photograph and trying its hardest to exude hatred even in his petrified state.

"Fuckin' hell," hissed Vilém, leaping back and wringing his arm, fearing that merely touching an image of the Nazi would infect him with whatever filthy disease had consumed the Butcher's soul.

"Bastard," he growled, glaring into the still eyes of Heydrich. Although he had (obviously) never been fond of the long-dead Nazi, his recent encounter with Raya had changed the dull, obligatory hatred he had once felt towards Heydrich into a personal fire. It was Heydrich's fault that poor, sweet girl had been forced to suffer so much.

Vilém stepped away from Heydrich's visage and glanced at the accompanying paragraph:

Reinhard Heydrich: The Butcher of Prague (1904-1942)
Dubbed "The Man with the Iron Heart" by Hitler himself,
Reinhard Tristan Eugen Heydrich was the head of the SD
(Sicherheitsdienst), a Nazi intelligence division tasked with
organizing the arrest and murder of the Third Reich's
enemies, political and racial. Heydrich was one of the
primary architects of the "Final Solution to the Jewish
Question." He was the chairman of the infamous Wannsee
Conference, a secretive meeting of German officials where
plans for the Holocaust were discussed and finalized.
Heydrich's brutality earned him the position of
Reichsprotektor of Nazi-occupied Czechoslovakia in
September of 1941.
Heydrich was responsible for mass-scale executions and
terror throughout Czechoslovakia, earning him the epithet
"The Butcher of Prague." He was assassinated by two
Czechoslovak agents, Jan Kubis and Jozef Gabčík, in 1942
during Operation Anthropoid. After Heydrich's demise, Hitler
ordered several reprisals that resulted in the deaths and
incarcerations of thousands of Czechs and Jews. Although
historians continue to debate whether or not his
assassination was worth the high cost, almost all agree that
he was one of the most evil men in the Third Reich.

"...and that's saying something," sighed Vilém, turning away from the Butcher of Prague's arrogant features and letting his eyes wander to another display.

A familiar face caught his eye: a man, barely younger than Heydrich, dressed in black SS garb with a severe look on his face. He, unlike Heydrich, did not look at the camera as he was photographed. Instead, his eyes (which were light-colored, though Vilém couldn't tell their exact shade from the black-and-white photograph) wandered to the left, as if someone standing beside the cameraman had caught his eye.

Vilém didn't need to read the blurb under the picture to know that the man was the Camp's Kommandant. He remembered him from Raya's memories. He scowled at the man for a moment before curiously reading the snippet.

The Kommandant

Hans Gerber (1909-1945)

Born to an upper-class couple, Hans Gerber joined the SS in late 1932. His enthusiasm and loyalty to the ideals of Adolf Hitler caused him to rise through the ranks swiftly, and in October 1941, Reichsprotektor Reinhard Heydrich made him the Kommandant of this small camp.

Gerber, a sociopath with a morbid fascination for photography, took many pictures of his grisly work. Survivors and witnesses would often describe how he would climb to the top of the watchtower and take pictures during executions. Though many of these pictures were destroyed during the war, many more remain and are currently on display throughout this memorial site. Hans Gerber committed suicide shortly before Soviet forces arrived at the campground in 1945.

Vilém almost sighed in disappointment. Baseline information, and little of it was new to him. He hadn't known the Kommandant's name before, but his wickedness and his fascination with photography had been impressed upon him by Raya. He shot a scowl at the Kommandant's frozen image and instantly shivered as a frosty breeze snaked up his spine. He looked over at the door and was surprised to see that it was closed.

He sat between Heydrich and Gerber's respective informational boards, keeping careful watch over the artifacts and occasionally hopping up to shoo away some kids who got too close and put their oily fingers on the glass.

Soon, however, the guests, polite and rude alike, skittered out of Barrack Four. One of Vilém's fellow guards stepped in to inform him that the Camp was closed.

"You good for the night?" he asked, and Vilém nodded.

"Good as ever," he replied.

"I'm locking up and leaving you with the ghosts, then. Night, Vilém."

"Night!" said Vilém, waving as his coworker exited the barrack. He perked up his ears and heard the Camp gate creak as it was shut.

"Well," Vilém sighed, patting his hands on his thighs and standing up, looking at the pictures of Heydrich and Gerber. "Looks like it's just you and me, guys. Fun times, huh?"

Obviously, neither Nazi said a thing.

"Right…" Vilém sighed. He exited Barrack Four to briefly patrol the rest of the Camp.

He returned after half an hour and instantly, a chill enveloped him. Not the chill he was accustomed to— the usual cold Czech air that sometimes passed through the thin wooden walls of the barracks. Yet it was still familiar. He had felt this before, even more strongly, when his fingers had brushed against the graffiti-clad wall of Barrack Five.

"Raya?" he whispered.

No familiar gentle voice replied, but the cold aura seemed to beckon him. He obeyed its wishes eagerly, thinking that perhaps Raya Pomnenka had returned to the campsite. He hoped that wasn't the case. The poor girl had seemingly moved on weeks ago, but her fractured memories might have hidden something from her. Perhaps she had remembered something and had returned to tell him before she faded for good.

"Raya? Raya, sweetie, is that you?"

The aura led him to one of the display cases in front of the Heydrich Exhibit.

His brow shot up. He was standing before a faded picture of a little boy. Some sort of notice. It was in German, and Vilém only knew a few words of German, so he couldn't quite tell what it said. The placard that accompanied it was not very helpful: *"Issue from Heydrich's Office, 1941."*

The aura continued to call to him, all but begging him to disobey Ms. Doubek and press his fingers against the glass. He sighed.

"Oh, you spirits are gonna get me fired," he

muttered, but he obeyed nonetheless, letting his oily fingers smudge the display case.

He stood still for a moment, waiting, then, remembering how he had communicated with Raya before, he shut his eyes.

"Hello?" he called into the darkness.

A voice replied: *H…Hallo…*

Not Raya's voice. Stronger than that of the shy girl, but also much younger. The spirit speaking with him now must have been no older than eleven. He was partially relieved that Raya was truly at peace and hadn't returned, but at the same time he was astonished and saddened at the revelation that she was not the only restless spirit tarrying at the Camp.

He smiled softly, although he wasn't sure if such a gentle gesture would even register to the ghost.

"Hi, sweetie," he said. "Are you lost? Do you have something you need to tell me?"

J-ja…Ich…tut mir leid…Ich spreche…Ich…I don't… Czech…don't speak well…

Vilém grunted softly. Well, that was going to make things even more difficult. He would not give up just because of a language barrier, of course, but it would still make it harder than it had been when he'd helped Raya.

It was odd, however: what was a German child doing here, in a concentration camp that, as far as he knew, had been built to house Czech "undesirables"? Their little camp was hardly Auschwitz—not the sort of camp he could imagine the Nazis would go out of their way to ship Jews to if it was inconvenient. And it certainly wouldn't have been convenient to ship Jews from the Sudetenland or Germany to this particular camp when there were several other camps they could have otherwise been sent to that would have been closer.

Interrogating the girl as to why she was here likely wouldn't do any good. Or, at least, a verbal interrogation wouldn't do any good.

"*Alles ist gut, alles ist gut, kleine,*" Vilém assured the girl with what little German he knew. "*Ich kann dich hilfe, Ich will dich hilfe.*"

Danke...du...you...Raya...helped...

"*Ja. Du weisst Raya?*"

Raya, yes...knew her. Bad memory. Not so with me. Good memory...I...good memory...not as Raya.

"That's good. Very good. *Sehr gut.* Can you show me your memory? Show? Make me see? Like Raya? *Wie Raya?*"

Ein moment, bitte...ein moment...

Being pulled into this little girl's memory was like riding a bike for the first time after abandoning it for a year: strange, a tad uncomfortable, but familiar all the same. In fact, though the deceased Jew's embrace was icy, like Raya's had been, it was much less so. There was a hint of warmth, of hope, that morose Raya had lacked. Perhaps, Vilém thought, this child's story wouldn't be as tragic.

Of course, he couldn't let his hopes get too high. This *was* the Holocaust he was quite literally delving into.

The transition to the ghostly memory-world was sudden. One moment he was standing by the Heydrich Exhibit, his oily fingers touching the glass that kept him from the unreadable official notice, and the next...well, the next he was seeing the world as it had been a lifetime ago, through the eyes of a little Jewish girl.

The girl was running through a wooded area. She glanced to her side and Vilém saw another girl, a child with wavy blonde hair tied into two clumsy pigtails and shimmering emerald eyes, dressed in a very nice white blouse and a blue skirt. His heart ached for a moment. She reminded him of his sisters when they were younger. She was six, maybe seven if he was being generous.

My sister...my twin. That's my sister. My sister is Ilona. I'm Iveta.

Well, then at least he could get an idea of what the little spirit speaking to him looked like. He didn't have a mirror around this time, but it was probably safe to assume they'd be identical. Iveta glanced down and dusted herself off, and Vilém realized she and her sister were dressed exactly the same.

"Twins..." Vilém muttered. "I see...so you two were very close then? What year is...?"

S-sorry...sorry...still having trouble...not understanding well....maybe watch only?

"Oh! Oh, sorry..."

Well, he thought, *I hope these memories come with subtitles.*

Fortunately, he quickly discovered that he wouldn't need subtitles. Iveta started to fall behind in what was evidently becoming a race between the twins and cried out: "Sis! C'mon, slow down!"

And although she surely must have spoken in German, Vilém understood it clear as day, as though it had been uttered in his own native Czech. He marveled at this for a moment, wondering why he could now understand German-speakers in a memory. In Raya's memory, he hadn't been able to understand what the Germans had said.

Then again, he reasoned, *she was Czech and didn't speak German. Since I was in her memory, of course I'd only understand what she understood. Maybe it's the same here: this is Iveta's memory, so I'll hear words the way she did and understand them as much as she could. It's not the same thing as a recording or a movie.*

He breathed a sigh of relief for the small blessing. Comprehending this memory would still likely be tougher since he didn't have the benefit of a verbose narrator, but at the very least he would understand what the twins said to each other.

"Ilona, please!"

"Slowpoke!" giggled Ilona. Iveta stumbled and almost collapsed, and Vilém felt himself totter just as she did. Just like before, Vilém would feel whatever the little girl felt. The wind in her face, the sweet smell of the trees tickling her nose, all sensations Iveta had experienced so long ago.

Iveta barely summoned the coordination to keep herself from falling flat on her face. She took a moment to regain her balance and looked up to see that her sister was gone.

"Ilona?" she cried, and Vilém felt the little girl's heart skip several beats as she trudged on, her eyes shifting wildly about the woods, searching for a sign of her sister.

"Ilona!" she cried, louder, her frightened voice

echoing out over the trees. In the distance, she heard her sister call to her, so far away that she couldn't even make out her words, only her teasing tone.

Vilém felt warm water build up behind Iveta's eyes, and as her eyes became foggy, he felt her heart palpitate. She couldn't see, couldn't see where her sister was. She was going to be trapped in the woods forever and starve and…

"Iva!"

Vilém felt a comforting little hand wrap around Iveta's wrist, and the sobbing girl (whose memories he could barely witness through the ocean of tears in her eyes) pliantly allowed her sister to lead her through the woods.

"You're so stupid, Iva!" sighed Ilona in an exasperated tone that made it clear this wasn't the first time this had happened.

"S-sorry…" hiccupped Iveta. They stopped and Vilém felt fondness warm his chest as Ilona reached up and wiped the tears from the corners of her twin's eyes with her thumb. Just like him and his little sisters: they could argue as often as they liked, tease each other until tears blinded their eyes, but they loved each other. He could feel that love nestled in Iveta's chest when her vision cleared and she saw her sister pouting in front of her.

"Damn it, Iveta," sighed Ilona. "You know if I wasn't around, you'd never survive these woods. You would'a been eaten by a wolf."

"P-probably…" muttered Iveta.

"And then what? The Star Shack would just go to

waste!" Ilona laughed, grabbing her sister's hand and dragging her out of the bushes.

Vilém wasn't sure what he had been expecting the girls to be running towards, but nonetheless he was surprised when Iveta blinked the tears from her eyes enough to view her surroundings.

They were in the midst of what looked like a long-abandoned wheat field. Shriveled stalks of grain wafted about in the breeze. A railroad track split the gray field in half and continued on into the woods, but it was so old—with tracks beginning to come up and metal bits rendered copper with rust twisting here and there—that Vilém suspected there hadn't been a train rolling on those tracks for years. Perhaps the First World War had disconnected the track from the rest of civilization.

Iveta's eyes only lingered on the tracks for a second before they shifted to their true destination.

At the edge of the dead field stood a watchtower, the sort that Vilém always saw near farmland, the sort hired hands rested in while guarding the crop. Vilém shivered when he saw it. He had once found such struc-tures innocuous, but working at the Camp had soured his perception of watchtowers.

Ilona grabbed her sister's hand and the twins jovially skipped towards the foreboding structure. Vilém real-ized that there was a sign hanging on the door, painted in a childish script that, even if the memory had given him the ability to read and comprehend German, likely would have been beyond his ability to decipher.

They entered the old watchtower, and Vilém almost chuckled when he realized the twins had transformed the abandoned building into some sort of clubhouse. They had placed pink cushions on the splintery wooden chairs, two violet sleeping beds lay on the floor, an army of stuffed animals was lined up on a desk, and the walls were decorated with their drawings.

Iveta inhaled deeply, and Vilém was grateful when she did so as he got to enjoy the most wonderful scent. Iveta turned towards a mountain of sacks stacked high in one corner of the hideaway. Although he didn't speak German, Vilém knew the word for "sugar", which was plastered all over a third of the bags. Sugar, flour, marshmallows, cookies. The girls had a stock of sweets fit for the apocalypse.

"Are we bringing anything back?" Ilona asked, darting to the stack of sugar sacks. "Flour? Sugar? What?"

"Nothin' this time," Iveta said, snatching a box of cookies and a blanket from the corner. "Mama said she's good for the week."

Iveta's spirit clumsily attempted to explain: *Ah...Mother...did...bakery...we keep things here for safety....many....much stealing in village...but nobody knows about clubhouse of Ilona and I.*

"I get it," Vilém said, though he could only barely comprehend what the girl was trying to tell him. He kept watching as Iveta gathered some books into her arms, catching a glimpse at the covers. Although he couldn't read the German, he could tell from the pictures of stars and celestial bodies on the front of the hardbacks that they were about astronomy.

"C'mon! The sun's gonna go down pretty soon!" Ilona yelled at her sister, causing Iveta's heart to race.

She looked over her shoulder so swiftly that her own pigtails smacked her in the eye and she yelped in pain, causing her twin to giggle.

"Klutz, you can hurt yourself with anything!" Ilona laughed.

Iveta mumbled something so quietly that even Vilém—despite being inside the girl's skull—couldn't decipher her words.

She grabbed a small pile of papers and three freshly-sharpened pencils before bolting up the bare-bones spiral staircase. Vilém could feel Iveta's thudding heart quicken its pace as she felt the stairs, half devoured by age and termites, creak loudly beneath her feet. To Vilém, it was a familiar nervousness, one that he had possessed when he was a boy climbing up the shaky rope ladder to Erik's treehouse. Frightened that today would be the day it broke, but having trusted it to bear the burden of his body so many times that doing so was practically instinct.

Iveta clambered eagerly through the trapdoor to the top floor of the watchtower, which her sister, seemingly without an iota of fear, had thrust open so roughly that the whole watchtower trembled.

"Ilona!" squeaked cautious Iveta. Ilona, unfazed, grabbed the books from her sister and flung herself onto a well-worn sleeping mat laid out beneath a hole in the watchtower's roof.

"Don't be such a baby, sis. C'mon, I wanna see Taurus!" Ilona said, holding a pencil in her teeth and flipping to a particular page in one hardback. Iveta heaved a disgruntled sigh, but Vilém felt forgiveness wash over the little girl's heart as she took a seat beside her sister.

Vilém, who had failed astronomy, could barely understand what the girls discussed with such breathless amazement for the rest of the night. Iveta would gesture to the stars and point out shapes and ancient figures that Vilém couldn't see. But even though he couldn't discern the figures in the sky, he felt sparks of fascination light up Iveta's mind. He felt her love for her sister, the joy she felt spending time with her, and a slight spark of pride. A spark whose presence could perhaps be explained by the fact that it seemed astronomy was Iveta's area of expertise.

"Trace it out, Ilona!" Iveta said, gesturing to the stars above, and Ilona happily complied, sketching out Taurus. For a young child, she had an older artist's hand.

The girls both laid back once their stargazing had tired their eyes out.

"Hey...Ilona…" Iveta muttered, and Vilém felt the girl's heart sink. "What're we gonna do when we're older and I go to college?"

Iveta's ghost spoke again. *Sister was good...with the cakes...the bakery...wanted to own as adult, not me, not good with art or icing, me. Wanted to astro....student, student be.*

Ilona, unperturbed, shrugged her twin's question off. "We'll still see each other," she assured her.

"There's no college in the village, Illa. I'm gonna have to go away…"

"We walk all the way out here every other night, Iva! I'm sure I'll be able to get to you. I'll make those cookies shaped like stars you like and deliver 'em.

Maybe I'll go to college. Baking college or art college. Dunno, but don't worry, I won't abandon you. Can't. You'd die if I did, klutz."

Ilona gave her sister what Vilém could tell was meant to be a light slap on the arm, but to delicate Iveta it felt like a boxer had punched her. She yelped and tears filled her eyes, clouding her vision, blinding her and Vilém.

Her vision suddenly cleared and Vilém was startled when he saw that the memory had shifted. No longer was Iveta in the watchtower; she was standing in a kitchen, sweat and tears covering her face. A woman knelt before her, scowling and shaking her head as she held out a hand.

"Let's see it," the woman said, and Iveta offered her arm, which was sporting a minor burn. The woman, presumably the twins' mother, clicked her tongue in disapproval.

"Silly girl, this is why I tell you to let Ilona handle the oven," she said.

"I was trying to make a surprise for her..." mumbled Iveta as her mother marched over to a cabinet and pulled out a roll of bandage tape. Iveta averted her gaze as her mother dressed her injury, her eyes falling upon her failed creation: a burnt cake that sat on a counter, surrounded by cans of icing. She must have burned herself taking it out of the oven: she hadn't been able to decorate it.

"I'm sure she'll appreciate you staying safe more than any cake, Iva," said the twins' mother, tightening the bandage and making her daughter squeal. Iveta's mother chuckled, reaching out with a flour-covered hand and pinching her daughter's cheek. Vilém could feel sticky batter cling to Iveta's face.

There was a *ring* from outside the kitchen, a telltale sign that someone had entered the bakery.

"Mama, it happened again!" Ilona's voice, filled with distress, rose above the slam of a door. Iveta's mother swore.

"Again…?" mumbled Iveta, and Vilém felt her heart tumble to the bottom of her stomach.

Her mother marched out of the kitchen like a hurricane and Iveta scuttled after her, running so quickly that Vilém only barely caught a glimpse of the family bakery: small, quaint, only enough space for two tables and a booth. The walls had been decorated with paper cut-outs of stars and planets, no doubt contributed by the little artist and the little astronomer.

"Let's go," huffed the twins' mother, slamming the door behind her, the bell jingling viciously in her wake. Ilona grabbed her sister's hand and the two stayed close to their mother, Iveta's heart pounding as they shuffled through the village. She looked side to side, earning scowls from her neighbors and rude gestures from a gaggle of teens.

Only Jews in town we were, the ghost explained. *Some fine with this, many not. My father…killed on way home from work…Jew-haters did…when very tiny me and Ilona were.*

"I'm so sorry…" Vilém muttered, watching as the family rounded a corner and arrived at a graveyard by a church. It didn't surprise him that the girls' father was buried in a church cemetery: their village was so tiny, and if they were the only Jews, there was no other place he could have been laid to rest.

He felt his anger spike when he saw where the Jewish man's grave was located: in a muddy corner far from where the gentiles were buried, as though the Christians of the village hadn't even wanted their dead to associate with a member of the Jewish race.

"I guess the Nazis didn't bring any new ideas here..." Vilém muttered, and he sensed bitter agreement emanating from Iveta's spirit.

As they got close to the isolated plot, Vilém realized what had "happened again." Someone had painted graffiti all over the headstone. It stood at an odd angle, as though the vandals had initially tried to knock it over and, upon being foiled, opted to deface it. Vilém couldn't read the graffiti, and when Iveta chose to read it aloud, he almost wished he had remained ignorant.

"'One Jew Down, Three to Go!'" the girl whimpered, and he felt her spine tingle as though a serpent had started slithering up her back.

Ilona's grip on her sister's hand tightened, a reassuring action that Vilém sensed Iveta appreciated.

"Childish nonsense, probably some teens," Iveta's mother said, squatting before her husband's grave and brushing her thumb over his name. "Don't you girls worry about it, not one bit..."

"They got Papa..." Iveta pointed out, her morose observation causing a cloud of fear to descend upon the family. The cloud parted, however, when Ilona hooked arms with her twin.

"I'll protect Iva!" Ilona volunteered. Their mother smiled.

"That's my brave girl...Iveta, don't worry, Ilona's got you. Nothing messes with Ilona."

"Hm..." muttered Iveta, looking towards her father's grave, her gut roiling as though she had eaten an expired pastry.

But suddenly, Ilona dangled a shiny something-or-other in front of her face. Iveta winced, but Vilém felt her fear transform into gratitude when her eyes focused on the object and she realized it was a bracelet.

"Surprise!" Ilona declared, grabbing her sister's arm. "Happy birthday! I made it for you, took me some time...I was just showing Papa. It's my best work, I think, even better than the cakes."

Ilona slipped the bracelet onto her sister's wrist and Iveta lifted her arm, holding the bracelet up to the sun. Golden star-shaped beads shimmered in the light, and a bead painted to look like the earth rested calmly beneath her thumb.

"Hey, what happened to your arm, sis?" Ilona queried, and Vilém felt Iveta's face heat up.

"Erm...I was trying to make your birthday present and I got burned...I didn't get to finish it...sorry..." muttered Iveta, fiddling with the beads on her birthday bracelet.

Ilona giggled. "You're silly! You don't know how to use the oven, you klutz! Next time for our birthday, just don't get hurt, okay? That's a good present."

"I was trying..." sighed Iveta.

"Well...that's good!" Ilona said, leaning forward and kissing her sister's cheek. Their mother smiled with fond sorrow at their affectionate display and then commanded Ilona to take her sister home while she handled the graffiti.

"See you back at the bakery, Mama!" Ilona cried,

leading her sister away from the graveyard. But despite all of Ilona's attempts to comfort and distract her sister, Iveta looked back, looked at the dire warning on her father's grave. Her head started spinning, her heart trembling, fear rushing through her veins. Tears blinded her again.

"Ilona, get away from the window!"

The memory shifted once more. Iveta and her mother were ducking behind the counter, peeking out just enough to see Ilona crouching by the front of the store. A yellow word, '*Jude*', had been painted on the bakery's window. Outside, a thick crowd had gathered. Had Vilém not known his history, he would have had no clue what the hubbub was about.

But the nearby calendar showed that it was October 1938. The Munich Betrayal had just happened. The Sudetenland belonged to Hitler, and the anti-Semites of Ilona and Iveta's hometown must have been welcoming the Nazi troops.

Iveta's mother crept out of her hiding place, wrapping her arm around her too-brave daughter's waist and slowly pulling her away from the window. Iveta watched. It seemed as though she was in a trance: her eyes were glazed over, her mouth ajar.

CRASH!

A hunk of brick shattered the thick glass and snapped Iveta out of her dreamlike state. Ilona screamed and clung to her mother. Shards stabbed their flesh and Vilém could feel Iveta's fear paralyze her.

Everything happened too fast. Before the glass could

even strike the floor, Iveta's mother ran to her other daughter and grabbed her hand. A mob pursued, screaming and hissing. Iveta's mother slammed the kitchen door shut and blocked it with a table. It wouldn't give her much time. Vilém knew that, and evidently so did Iveta's mother. She took her girls and dragged them to the closest hiding place: a massive oven. Vilém felt his heart sink at the irony. The scent of char and ash assaulted Iveta's sinuses as she and her sister were pushed in.

"Stay quiet!" their mother warned them, slamming the door, and Ilona slapped a hand over Iveta's mouth. Vilém could tell that such a gesture was unnecessary. Iveta was too frightened to move or make a noise.

She sat there, the grate digging into her hands and bottom, listening to her sister's quiet, hopeless assurances that everything would be okay. She saw nothing, but heard everything. The door flying open. Her mother pleading for mercy. "Dirty Jew," being screeched by the neighbors. She heard her mother call out names, perhaps recognizing formerly friendly faces in the mob, but all masks had been pulled off and there was no mercy.

She heard her mother screaming. She heard laughing. She smelled skin burn.

And when there was finally silence, they lingered in the oven. They waited and waited until they could stand it no more. Iveta stretched her foot out and nudged the oven door open. Cautiously, the girls crawled out.

Iveta let her eyes flit to and fro. The bakery was in ruins, looted to the point where only a few rusty pots and pans and some baking supplies were left behind.

"Mama…?" Ilona whispered, and the twins searched for their mother.

Iveta peeked behind an upturned table and screamed. Vilém felt horror strangle her soul when she saw what had become of her mother.

A burned mound of flesh and tattered fabrics covered in blackened blood was all that remained. At first it seemed she was dead, and Vilém would have thought it better if that were true, but her chest rose and fell. Though her eyes had been pulled from her head, her fingernails torn off, her skin scorched, and though all she could do was blindly twitch, she lived. The mob had stopped just short of murder. Perhaps they thought it better to let her die blind, slow, in agony, alone.

She wasn't alone, but her daughter couldn't look at her. Iveta turned away and vomited all over the blood-stained floor. Ilona approached, and Iveta, still heaving and sobbing, barely saw her sister's expression shift from horror to sorrow before it settled on a frightening stoniness.

"She's alive…" Ilona muttered, walking to her mother's side. "Mama, can you hear me?"

Her mother did not indicate that she could. Iveta dared look at what remained of her mother once more, and Vilém could sense that she was grateful for the tears obscuring her view of the almost-corpse.

"We…we've gotta get her help, a doctor…" whimpered Iveta, and Ilona's eyes, full of fire, narrowed at her sister.

"The doctors are the ones who did this to her,"

Ilona said. "We're on our own. Nobody's gonna help us. Nobody cares."

Straightening up, Ilona stepped away from her mother, tip-toeing over glass and bricks until she reached a drawer. She opened it.

"They didn't take everything, good." She drew two sharp, shiny knives from the drawer and offered one to her sister. Iveta gingerly took it, staring inquisitively up at her severe sister.

"Ilona…?"

"We're alone, Iva," Ilona said. "We'll have to run for the Star Shack."

"And…then what?"

"Grow up, and then we'll come back and kill everyone here, everyone who did this to Mama," Ilona declared, one trembling hand twirling the knife, gently stabbing at the air, as though she was imagining their tormentors before her, as though the empty space was their flesh.

A sob choked Iveta. "I don't wanna kill anyone!" she insisted, but her sister ignored her. Ilona, whose eyes seemed to have aged fifty years, turned her gaze towards what remained of their mother.

"We gotta, though…" Ilona muttered, and although Vilém immediately knew what she was talking about, he felt confusion bubble up in Iveta's brain.

"W…wha…?"

"Mama…we can't leave her like this."

"Illa…no…"

"There's nobody to help her, she's hurting…"

"No, no, **no!**"

"Shhh, Iva, keep your voice down or they'll hear us!

They'll come back! They'll do it to us too!" hissed Ilona, towering over her sister. Iveta sobbed, shook her head, and dropped the knife. It clattered to the ground, landing in a puddle of blood and splashing a few droplets onto Ilona's ankles.

"I can't, I can't..." whimpered Iveta, feeling as though she was going to vomit again.

"You're not brave enough, I know..." whispered Ilona. "It's fine. I'll be brave for both of us. Give her a kiss goodbye."

Iveta glanced at her mother's peeling onyx skin, and Vilém could feel her stomach churn at the thought. He could feel guilt slash at her gut, attacking her for being so disgusted by her own mother, but she couldn't help it. She shook her head and hid her face in her hands.

"It's fine...." whispered Ilona again. "Fine, you're not brave enough. I'll be brave for you, Iva."

Iveta was crying so much that even if she had looked up, she likely wouldn't have been able to see through her tears. But she heard Ilona's footsteps daintily march towards the half-dead woman. She heard her twin whisper her final goodbyes and declarations of love to their mother. She heard her plant a bold kiss on her mother's cheek.

Iveta dared to look up, dared to let her tear-filled eyes fall upon her sister as she raised the knife.

Something wrong, someone here...

The ghost interrupted, and just as Ilona plunged the knife downwards, Vilém suddenly found himself back in Barrack Four, falling backwards, as though he had been shoved out of the spirit's memories.

Vilém yelped as he landed hard on the dusty

barrack floor, but he wasn't a weak man and it would take more than a fall to stun him. He immediately hopped back to his feet and slapped his hand on the display case, nearly knocking it over in his haste.

"Iveta?! Iveta, what happened? Are you still there, are you all right?!"

A chilly gust of wind tickled his ear, but he didn't hear the girl's voice. He set about touching every object in the Heydrich Exhibit, but nothing summoned the ghost once more.

By the time he had touched every inch of Barrack Four, day broke and a coworker came in to relieve him of his shift.

"Jesus, man, you okay?" the day guard asked as he shooed Vilém out of the barrack and saw the worry spilling from his coworker's eyes. "Ya' look like you saw a ghost."

FOR THE NEXT FEW DAYS, Vilém didn't see or hear any ghosts, and he never would have thought that an absence of paranormal activity would distress him so greatly.

That Ms. Doubek didn't fire him after he left a criminology database's worth of fingerprints all over absolutely everything in the Heydrich Exhibit demonstrated that she had more mercy in her old, shriveled heart than she let on. Still, she warned him to stop touching everything.

"Don't know why you'd want to anyway...." she

grumbled. "All this shit from the Butcher...even *I* don't want to get near it, much less touch it."

But he kept at it, night after night, the silence of Barrack Four tormenting him. He searched the other barracks, but he could find no sign of either Iveta or the entity that had frightened her.

Perhaps it was his latent paternal instincts kicking in, but he couldn't get the poor girl out of his head. So little and frightened and stuck in that damn camp for God knows how long. He could barely eat, barely sleep, and going out with Erik or planning something fun with Jana...he couldn't. The idea of going out and having fun and living when that poor child was still suffering made guilt tie his stomach into knots.

He looked up everything he could about ghosts, doing his best to separate the bull from what sounded like potential truth. Unsurprisingly, there was a lot of bull, and soon he gave up on the internet and decided there was nothing he could do.

He felt like he had when he was a little boy and his cat would tarry on her daily hunts. He would be at home waiting by the door, knowing there was nothing he could do, but too worried to do anything but sit on the porch and wait.

A week of hermitude went by, and one day, he got a text.

Erik: Hey bro, you ok?

He sighed and decided not to leave his friend hanging.

Vilém: Yeah, man. Just kinda in one of those moods.

Erik: Y'know that Jana girl's been texting you. I met her at the bar the other day and she said you won't answer.

Vilém felt guilt prick his soul. He liked Jana, and he would have been content to text her all day and night, but that was the problem. It would have made him content. He felt so spoiled, having the option to go out and have fun while Iveta languished. He was privileged enough to live in a time where he would never have to dream of mercy killing his own mother. Why did he deserve such a cozy, happy life when little Iveta didn't even get a peaceful death?

He chewed on his lip and considered lying to his friend, but he felt like his chest would explode if he kept holding everything in and decided to be reasonably earnest.

Vilém: We got a new exhibit at the Camp. I don't know, man, I think that place is getting to me again. I'm seeing these little kids dying and stuff every night and then I feel guilty wanting to go out and just have fun. It's like...if they didn't get a chance at that, why do I deserve it?

Vilém: Sorry, rambling.

Erik: Hey bro, believe it or not, I totally know where you're coming from. You remember my mom?

Vilém shuddered. He knew Erik would never bring up his mother unless it was a genuine friend emergency. Erik's mother had been an absolute nightmare, a soul without a drop of humor, even worse than Ms. Doubek. Vilém had never seen her smile.

Vilém: How could I forget?

Erik: You remember what she used to say to me whenever we got into trouble or I got a bad grade?

Vilém: "Your grandma didn't survive Auschwitz just for her only grandson to ____"

Erik: Lol, yup. But you know my grandma, she was the best. And I always kind of wondered, "Why is it that my grandma is literally awesome and enjoys life even after going through Auschwitz, but my mom, who didn't have to deal with any of that, acts like the whole world's a cesspit?"

Vilém: And what's your hypothesis?

Erik: Same thing you're going through right now. It's like a weird generational survivor's guilt. Grandma went through hell, she lost everything, and I bet every time Mom tried to do anything, she had Auschwitz on the mind.

Erik: My mom loved Grandma, and I bet she was always thinking, "Why do I deserve to have fun and be a kid if my mom had to go through Auschwitz?" And then after I was born, same thing got foisted onto me. And you know my mom was never happy about anything, and you know my grandma hated that. She tried to give Mom a good life after what she went through, and Mom appreciated it in the wrong way.

Erik: I guess what I'm kinda trying to say is: don't be like my mom, man. You're great, and all those good people you feel guilty for, they wouldn't want ya' to make yourself miserable because they were miserable. Like my grandma. They'd want you to appreciate what

they went through and be happy on
their behalf.

Erik: Like my grandma used to say:
every time a Czech or Jew smiles,
Hitler turns in his grave.

Erik: So what I'm basically saying
is: text Jana, you fuck, or I'm
gonna steal her.

Vilém laughed, his heart lighter than it had been in
a week.

Vilém: Ok, I'll text her right now.
Thanks, bro, I knew there was a
reason I'm still your friend.

Erik: Well, I DO still have those
pictures from Christmas.

Vilém: Delete those. Now.

Erik: Fuck no, you know too much
about me. I need blackmail material
of my own.

Vilém: Fine, but I reserve the
right to tell the slug story if
those pictures ever leak.

Erik. That's mutually assured

> **destruction, dude. That's what friendship is.**
>
> **Vilém: TTYL, bro, I've gotta write an apology novel to Jana. Wanna do something stupid next weekend?**
>
> **Erik: Prague?**
>
> **Vilém: Prague.**
>
> **Erik: Prague next weekend. Plan made.**

Vilém switched to Jana's number. After he apologized for ghosting her and she forgave him, they made a plan to meet on Saturday. They exchanged some goofy texts and by the time Vilém set off for work, he was wearing the biggest, dumbest grin in the world. It felt like he had cast off a heavy weight. He felt happy, and even better, he didn't feel bad for feeling happy.

He got to the Camp, received his nightly lecture from Ms. Doubek, and then returned to Barrack Four with a newfound sense of hope. The Camp cleared out, and almost as soon as he was alone, he felt a familiar presence lingering by the poster in the Heydrich Exhibit. His heart somersaulted and he slammed his hand against the display case.

"Iveta?" he yelled, squeezing his eyes shut.

Seem...happier, you are...very good! The girl's spirit sounded much more cheerful than he would have expected given the circumstances. *Very no happy you were, all week. Thought you felt it too.*

"Felt what?"

Bad spirit somewhere here, can sense. Nazi maybe? Cannot tell, cannot find, but you must...careful, very careful be...don't want you to hurt.

"I'll be careful," he assured the girl, sounding much braver than he was. A Nazi spirit? He supposed it only made sense: if a Jew could linger, so could a Nazi. He remembered being in Prague and sensing an angry presence near the spot where Heydrich had died.

Perhaps Heydrich had attached himself to one of his old possessions. Vilém grunted. Fantastic, just what he *didn't* need: the ghost of the Architect of the Holocaust trouncing about his workstation.

He decided he would have to deal with one ghost at a time, however, and smiled at the invisible presence.

"Don't worry about me, Iva, whatever it is. Let's focus on you: what happened to you after the Bakery Incident?"

Ilona and I ran to Star Shack. Had food. Survived okay for very long. Nobody find for long time until one day...

Vilém felt his stomach lurch once more, like a roller coaster had taken off, and before he knew it, he was once again in Iveta's memories.

"Iva, there's a boy outside."

Iveta's eyes, bleary from sleep, slowly opened. Ilona was standing above her, three years older than she had been on that day in the bakery. Even though she was a mere ten years old, she had the eyes of a woman. Her clothes were much more ragged compared to what Iveta was wearing, indicating that she braved the outside world more often than her sister. Behind her, a mountain of flour and sugar still stood. It seemed that the stock had been serving the girls well for the duration of the occupation.

Iveta raised her hand up to rub her eyes, the star bracelet shimmering on her wrist as she did so. She hadn't been doing much for her own personal hygiene, but she must have made certain to clean that bracelet every day.

"...A...what...?"

"Boy. He's blonde. Looks like a gentile." Ilona held up the knife she had used on their mother. Rust-colored stains clung to the once shimmering surface of the blade. "I'm gonna go kill him."

That woke Iveta up. She sprung to her feet and grabbed her twin's wrist. "Wait! Illa, what if he's a Jew?"

"Don't look like one..."

"Neither do we! Where is he?"

"Lyin' on the tracks outside."

"The tracks?"

"Come up," Ilona commanded, and Iveta obeyed, cautiously following her sister up the unstable spiral staircase and shoving her way into the tower.

She looked down at the dead field. Indeed, on the abandoned tracks, she could see a tiny figure, a little boy. It was difficult to discern very much from so far away, but she saw golden hair, and when she squinted she saw something yellow on his shirt. Vilém knew what that meant, and fortunately the girls had not isolated themselves so thoroughly that they didn't.

"I think he's wearing one of those yellow star thingies," Iveta said. "Like we saw when we snuck into the village. We saw that order, they're making the Jews wear them."

"Hm..." Ilona pursed her lips together in a thin, suspicious line.

"It'd be nice, y'know," Iveta muttered. "To know another Jew. We've only ever had each other."

"What's wrong with that?" Ilona snapped.

"Nothin', but more friends would be nice."

"Another mouth to feed."

"Another soldier," Iveta said, and Vilém almost chuckled. It seemed that Iveta knew exactly how to appeal to her vengeful twin. Ilona's eyes brightened.

"I guess...a boy may be useful."

"I'll go talk to him. You'll scare him if you march up to him with a knife."

"You *are* the friendly one," Ilona conceded, at last allowing a smile to tug at her lip. "I'll keep watch. But take your knife with you."

"All right..." sighed Iveta. She carefully maneuvered back downstairs, pausing by her cot to grab her knife, which was shiny and unused. She tucked it into her pocket and ran outside, slowing her jog as she drew close to the tracks.

The boy, whom Vilém immediately realized was the same child from the poster in the Heydrich Exhibit, looked worse for wear. About nine years old, with golden hair and aquamarine eyes that shimmered with somber thoughtfulness. Well-fed, though even from a moderate distance she could hear his stomach rumbling. His pale skin was marred with dirt and bruises. His black sweater, which looked lovingly hand-knitted, was torn and stained. A big, yellow six-pointed star bearing a crudely drawn word, '*JUDE*', was proudly sewn onto his chest. It looked like he'd made it himself.

"Uhm…" Iveta started to say, and the boy winced, sitting up. He made no attempt to run, but the fear that spewed from his eyes when they fell upon the skinny wastrel that was Iveta was so palpable it was practically contagious. Iveta felt a shiver go up her spine, but nonetheless she attempted to smile.

"Uh…what're you doing out here?" she asked. The boy took in a deep breath and fell back onto the tracks, facing the sky with a scowl, as though something about his current circumstance had made him mad at the heavens.

"Killing myself," he replied in a tone that would not have been inappropriate for a bored pupil describing his least favorite class.

"Oh…" Iveta replied, playing with her bracelet to distract herself from the uncomfortableness of this encounter. The boy stretched his hand out towards the sky and wiggled his fingers, letting the light strike his face in different spots.

"Sorry," he said, purposefully letting the sun attack his eyes. "I didn't know anyone else was out here. I'll move…"

"It doesn't really matter anyway," Iveta said. She pointed down the train tracks, which disappeared into the foliage, and explained, "The train tracks end down there; trains don't come through here anymore. You're not gonna get hit by anything."

The boy sat upright and looked down the tracks, pricking his ears up as though he hoped to hear the roar of an engine. The only noise that greeted him, however, was the twitter of birds. He groaned, slapped his hands over his face, and fell onto his side.

"Damn..." the child hissed. Iveta stepped over the metal edge of the train tracks and sat beside the boy, her hand hovering above his blonde head. Vilém sensed her empathetic hesitancy: it was as though she would have liked to comfort him, but wasn't sure if he would reject her touch.

She heard a snarl that made her wince, and she smiled when she realized it was merely the boy's stomach.

"You don't have to kill yourself, y'know. That won't make anything better," Iveta said. "My sister and me, we're Jews too, and we lost our family. If you're alone and your family's dead, you should come with us and one day we can all get our revenge together."

The boy laughed, and Vilém had never heard a child laugh the way he did. Bitter as a rotten apple, that laugh. It wasn't a laugh that should have come from an innocent boy.

But he laughed and laughed until he was crying. Iveta slowly stood, and Vilém could sense her concern. She must have thought he was mad, and Vilém wouldn't have blamed her one bit for assuming that.

Finally, the boy stopped laughing. He wiped the tears from his face and stood up. He must have been weak from not eating for God-knows-how-long; he stood with all the grace of a newborn goat, legs wobbling and almost collapsing beneath him. Iveta swooped in and saved him from falling, draping his arm over her shoulders.

"You need to come inside! We can give ya' something to eat," she said.

"I don't wanna steal your food," the boy said, helplessly stumbling along as the girl dragged him back towards her safehouse.

"We have tons of food, it's no big deal," Iveta assured him. "My sis and I have been out here for years. Don't worry about us. You look almost dead."

"That's the idea…" mumbled the boy.

"It's a bad idea, that's just what the gentiles want," Iveta said. "They want us to be hungry and miserable and dead! Don't do their job for 'em!"

"You're nice," the boy said, smiling at her, his eyes clouded. "You don't deserve to be out here all alone…"

"Not alone! Ilona, the boy's sick and hungry, get him something!"

Iveta nudged the door to the Star Shack open with her foot and called to her sister. Ilona came rushing down the stairs so fast that Vilém was surprised they didn't crumble under her feet. Iveta lay the boy down on her sleeping mat and ran to grab him something to eat. She smirked when she heard Ilona interrogating him.

"You have any friends?"

"I thought I did, but I think I was wrong," the boy replied, tugging on a loose thread on the mat. Iveta knelt by his side and offered him a loaf of bread, observing his angry fidgeting with a gentle smile.

"Our neighbors all betrayed us too, don't feel bad," Iveta said. Ilona shushed her.

"What's your name?" she asked. The boy nibbled on the bread, his blue eyes brightening.

"Klaus," he answered. He held up the loaf. "This is good!"

"We made it," Iveta said proudly, gesturing to the stock of wheat and flour behind them. "Not easy without an oven, but we manage!"

"Any siblings? Where's your mother? Where's your father?" Ilona asked. Klaus almost coughed up his bread at the word "father."

"My dad's gone," he said, and Iveta looked towards her sister, silently pleading for her to offer empathy. She was grateful when Ilona's stony eyes softened.

"Ours too, and our mom," Ilona said. "Eat something. You can stay here if you want."

Klaus offered Ilona what was left of his bread.

"I'm not hungry," he insisted weakly.

"Yes, you are. Eat," Ilona commanded, and after being harangued by both sisters for the better part of an hour, Klaus finally finished the one little piece of bread.

"If you're smart, you'll stay here," Ilona said. "You're welcome to. If you still wanna kill yourself, fine, but don't do it here or you may lead some Nazis right to us. Get your strength back and then go far, far away, and if you're captured, die and don't say anything about where we are. Got it?"

Klaus nodded, and Vilém could feel Iveta's heart plunge at the notion of letting the boy go off to his death. Vilém felt a wave of affection wash over him: poor Iveta was a sweetheart despite everything, caring so much for a boy she didn't even know.

Ilona announced that Klaus could do as he liked and climbed back up to keep watch, no doubt making sure the boy hadn't been followed. Iveta stayed by their exhausted guest's bedside, chatting with him. Klaus, perhaps unsurprisingly, wasn't in the mood for small talk, but he listened with a smile as Iveta explained how she and her sister had been living independently for so long.

"You two are really brave, living out here by yourselves," he said. Iveta fiddled with her star bracelet and shook her head.

"Ilona's the brave one. I'm just...here. I'm lucky to have her."

"You walked out to see me, that was pretty brave," Klaus pointed out, at last offering her a genuine, wide smile. He had one of the nicest smiles Vilém had ever seen, dimples decorating his rosy cheeks. Iveta tried and failed to suppress a blush.

"Nice one, Klaus, getting older girls..." Vilém joked, and Iveta's spirit laughed.

Liked him very much, Klaus. Klaus was very nice. Stayed for two weeks, hoped I...hoped he would stay forever...

"So...what happened to him?" Vilém asked, and although the Iveta of the past was chipper as she spoke to a smiling Klaus, the memory became cloudy and warped, as though the spirit herself was crying. When it cleared, the memory had once again shifted.

"Iva, get up, it snowed!"

Iveta evidently wasn't used to being roused with such enthusiasm. She screamed, and Vilém felt the word "Gestapo!" escape her lips before she sat up and realized it was only Klaus. The beaming boy had clumps of snow clinging to his shoulders and golden hair, but when his cheerful announcement was met with instinctual fear, his sweet smile turned sour.

"Sorry..." Klaus said. "Just wanted to let ya' know it snowed...Ilona's not really...uhm..."

He looked at Iveta's twin, who was fiddling with a box of matches. Ilona scoffed and lit the fireplace.

"Klaus, you need to quit being such a kid," Ilona sighed, and Vilém felt a dagger of sorrow strike his heart. What a thing for a ten-year-old to say.

"Hey, y'know...if you guys just...sit around and act miserable all day...well, that's just what the Nazis want. Miserable Jews," Klaus reasoned. He offered Iveta a hand, and Vilém could feel the shy girl's soul stir with eagerness as she grabbed it and let him drag her towards the door.

"Let's go play! Bet I could beat you in a snowball fight!" Klaus dared her, a mischievous glow conquering his aquamarine eyes.

Iveta hesitated only long enough to look towards Ilona. Her twin obviously thought it foolish, to go out and possibly get sick just for the sake of play, but she nonetheless waved for Iveta to go and have fun.

Vilém had never enjoyed a Holocaust memory so much. He remembered being a child, running around the woods and losing snowball fights to Erik. He had always wished he could experience those memories again, and through Iveta, for a short time, he did. Klaus was a brutal snowball fighter, showing no mercy despite his opponent being a girl. He defeated her, but he was a gracious victor, shaking hands over their snow peace treaty and even letting her keep half her territory.

Neither of them were dressed for the snow, but they stayed out, building a faceless snowman, creating snow angels, trying to knock icicles off the Star Shack. They played for hours, and Vilém almost forgot where he was. Iveta was so happy that the warmth in her heart made her feel toasty even as her fingers turned blue.

They finally became too tired to play anymore, but they didn't go back inside. Vilém could sense guilt growing in Iveta's chest, and though he didn't know the cause, he could assume she didn't want to return to her too-grown-up twin. She wanted to be a child, even if only for a few hours, and felt guilty about abandoning her sister for fun. She fiddled with her star bracelet and looked at Klaus, who was building a small, odd-shaped figure in the snow.

"What's that, Klaus?" asked Iveta. She looked at her friend's face and Vilém felt a sting in the girl's heart when she saw his forlorn expression.

"A bear..." Klaus answered. He smiled wistfully, his eyes becoming misty with nostalgia. "I had a white teddy bear...my papa got it for me. He took me skiing once, just him and me and my uncle. We played in the snow and he helped me ski...and when it was all over, he bought me a bear at the gift shop. I named it Heldi."

"'Hero'?" Iveta helpfully translated.

"I named it after Papa. He always picked me up if I hurt, but he didn't treat me like a baby. He let me get up myself..."

He stared down at the snow teddy bear for a moment, tears trailing down his ice-nipped cheeks.

"He really was my hero..." Klaus whispered.

"I'm sorry, Klaus..."

"Don't be...it's not your fault." He smiled at her, wiping his tears away with his snow-coated sleeve. "I know about your mom, but what about your dad?"

"He was Czech, I know that. He died before the Nazis came. Someone in the village killed him for being a Jew. I was little...I don't remember him much. I think Ilona remembers him better. He used to smoke a pipe...I remember the smell. And...I remember he'd do this thing where he held us both under his arms and he'd twirl us around and we'd pretend we were airplanes..."

Klaus laughed, but as he laughed, he seemed to cry as well. Tears rolled down his face, hiccups rocked his little body. His laughs died away and he sobbed.

"Papa did the same thing with me and my brother...the same thing," Klaus whimpered. "I don't understand...I don't understand...it doesn't make sense..."

"No...it doesn't," Iveta agreed. They sat still for a moment, sobs wracking the little boy's body. But suddenly, Klaus stood up, red-rimmed eyes wide, ears pricked up like a deer that had just heard a wolf howl.

"Klaus, what?"

"They're here...damn, I knew I shouldn't have stayed this long."

"Klaus...?"

"Shhh! Get down!"

He grabbed her by one of her pigtails, and Vilém was impressed that despite the sudden, painful tug on her hair, Iveta managed to keep herself from crying out as Klaus pulled her behind one of their snow forts. Klaus poked a small peephole in the icy structure and peeked at the woods.

"Shit..." the boy whispered, leaning away from the hole and gritting his teeth. Iveta shoved her eye into the hole and whimpered when she saw dark figures emerging from the thicket.

"Nazis…" she whimpered.

"SS," Klaus clarified. "They're combing the woods, looking for Jews. Iveta…"

He grabbed her by the shoulders and spun her around, forcing her to look into his eyes. His irises were colder and more intense than a blizzard. There was something strange about the child's eyes right then, something familiar.

"Run back to the watchtower! I'll lead them away from this place. I never should have stayed this long…"

"Klaus, no!" Iveta hissed, grabbing his hand as he started to stand and pulling him back down to safety. "They'll kill you, Klaus!"

"Good," Klaus said, and Vilém had never seen a nine-year-old with such a grim expression. There was no sign of sadness, however. Just acceptance, almost eagerness, as though he was about to give an old bully a kick to the balls.

"Klaus…"

"It's okay, Iveta." He offered her a smile. "It was nice to meet you. I wasn't wrong. You guys don't deserve any of this."

"Wha…?" Vilém felt confusion whirl through Iveta's brain, but before she could ask a question, Klaus leapt over the snow fort like a WWI soldier vaulting into No-Man's-Land. He screamed and waved his arms, and the Nazis rushed towards him. He led them away from the Star Shack.

Iveta squatted behind the snow fort for a moment, shell-shocked, but Klaus' sacrificial cry rang in her ears.

She skittered back to the Star Shack, kicking down the door and slamming it shut behind her.

"Ilona! Ilona! Put the fire out! The Nazis are here!" she shouted. Ilona cursed and stomped the fire into cinders. Iveta was sobbing uncontrollably, covering her face with both hands, desperately trying to silence herself.

"Where's the boy?" snapped Ilona, kneeling by the window and stealing a peek at the outdoors. Iveta lingered by the door. Her conscience begged her to be brave and stay by her sister, but her twisting throat and churning gut kept her frozen in place, muffling her own sobs with her fist.

"Klaus...led them...away..." she sobbed. Ilona scowled, holding her knife and waiting. Iveta stood still, staring at her sister, admiration blooming in her chest. Brave Ilona. Where would she be without her? She felt ashamed of herself right then. *Coward.* She was a coward. Always depending on Ilona to save her. Letting Klaus rush to his death for her.

Coward. Vilém could feel the word pounding against Iveta's ears even as her sister announced that the Nazis were approaching the Shack.

Coward. It echoed in her eardrums as her sister grabbed her hand and started dragging her up the stairs, vowing that they would be fine. She would surprise the Nazis. She would slit their throats. She would protect Iveta.

Coward. Iveta felt her sister's hand. It was trembling. Ilona was quaking. She was terrified.

Coward. They were almost at the top of the stairs when the word in her mind became a dare. Ilona was terrified, and still she acted brave. Iveta was only a coward because she did nothing.

Coward. Coward. Stop letting everyone else sacrifice for you. Coward...

"I'm not gonna be a coward anymore..."

"What...?"

"Ilona..." Iveta stopped and pulled her hand away once Ilona was safely off the unstable spiral staircase and in the observation deck. She stepped back and her twin gazed down at her with confused exasperation.

"Smile, please, Illa..." Iveta begged. "I miss your smile."

Ilona blinked in surprise and tightened her lips as though to resist the request, but it seemed to dawn on her that this odd desire was innocent and dire. She obeyed, forcing her lips upwards into a cruel mockery of what had once been a lovely smile.

"Keep smiling, Illa," Iveta begged.

"Iveta, wha...?"

But before Ilona could complete her query, Iveta leapt into the air.

"IVETA, NO!"

Too late. Iveta came down hard on the staircase, and the rotting wood crumbled. She crashed through stair after stair, obliterating the path to her sister as she fell.

CRASH!

Vilém fell back, yelping as he almost smashed right into Reinhard Heydrich's old fencing saber. He steadied himself as the pain from Iveta's memory sent him tumbling into the real world. His every bone felt phantom aches, and he took a moment to recover before standing up and valiantly pressing his hand against the glass once more.

"Sorry," he said to the spirit. "That was...a lot. I guess it didn't kill you, though."

No, no kill. Ilona was safe, though. Nazis not bother with broken stairs for one Jew only. That made me happy. But Nazis got me and Klaus...

"Klaus survived too?" Vilém exclaimed. "Lucky kid."

Nazis almost kill him, but...well...lucky...maybe not...

Vilém felt bitter tears sting his eyes. In the blink of an eye, he found himself in a new memory. Klaus was squatting in front of Iveta, his face barren as he signed his name on her cast-bound leg. For having been apprehended by the Nazis, he was in fairly good condition. Only a few cuts on his face and a slightly swollen eye. He drew a small heart on Iveta's cast right next to his name.

"There..." sighed Klaus. He and Iveta were sitting in what must have been the coziest jail cell in all the Third Reich: a couch, a cot, a little table with a platter of untouched food. A Nazi soldier stood by the door, scowling at the children. Klaus stood up and tossed the marker at the SS officer.

"I'm done with this," he announced. The Nazi grumbled and stooped down, picking up the marker.

"Little shit," Iveta heard the Nazi hiss. If Klaus heard that remark, he chose to ignore it, instead staring down at his friend's cast.

"Are you feeling any better?" Klaus asked. Iveta shrugged.

"I'm confused," Iveta said. "Maybe the Nazis are not as bad as we thought?"

"Not as bad, sure…" sneered Klaus, sarcasm dripping from his voice. He strutted towards the Nazi guard, crossing his hands behind his back and holding his head up imperiously.

"I'm thirsty," Klaus said.

"Good for you," snarled the Nazi.

"Go get me something to drink, you ugly idiot," the boy commanded, and Iveta's jaw dropped. Was he mad?

"And something for my friend too. I think hot chocolate would be nice," Klaus added, gesturing to the injured girl. The guard scoffed.

"You really think we're going to waste chocolate on a little Jewess?"

"What's your name?" Klaus queried, and Iveta's head spun with wonder when she saw sweat break out on the Nazi's brow. A small standoff ensued between the tiny boy and the Aryan soldier, Klaus' river-blue eyes freezing into icy pools as he stared the SS man into submission.

"With marshmallows?" the Nazi queried.

Klaus smirked. "Lots," he said, and Iveta could only sit there, completely baffled, as the Nazi left and brought back two mugs of marshmallow-filled hot chocolate. Klaus snatched them from the SS man and sat beside Iveta, giving her a mug. It smelled divine: she almost burned her tongue, she was so desperate to taste chocolate again.

"Klaus, why'd he listen to you?" Iveta whispered.

"He's afraid," Klaus replied, not drinking his own hot chocolate. He stared at the steam that rose from the cup, his eyes watering.

"Afraid of you? You're just a Jew, Klaus, why would he be afraid of you?"

"You'll see…" the boy whispered. The children sat in silence for some time. Iveta finished her hot chocolate and Klaus gave her his and took her empty mug, hugging it to his chest. Just as Iveta was lapping up the last drop of Klaus' drink, she heard chaos erupt in the hall outside their cell.

"Reichsprotektor's here!" one Nazi shouted, and the SS soldier guarding the children started shaking in his jackboots. Vilém felt Iveta's heart sink. She must have heard all about the Reichsprotektor, the Blonde Beast, and what he did to her people.

"Heydrich…" she whimpered. Klaus inhaled deeply, wiping the tears from his eyes and slowly setting the empty mug on the floor. He stood up, straightening the yellow star on his chest.

Their guard threw open the door and thrust his arm into the air. "Heil Hitler!" he barked.

Reinhard Heydrich entered, not bothering to greet the guard. Seeing the Blonde Beast in color was strange for Vilém, who had only ever seen him in pictures, in black-and-white like the monsters in old classic movies. But there he was, alive, real, clad head-to-toe in Nazi regalia, hair golden, eyes river-blue, his face…

Vilém and Iveta both felt confusion in unison. The Blonde Beast was wont, in pictures at least, to wear a wintry expression, at most an arrogant sneer. But standing before her right then, he looked like he had just narrowly dodged a bullet and was almost finished counting his lucky stars. Fear and relief gushed from Heydrich's eyes as they fell upon little Klaus.

Vilém realized before Iveta did that the Blonde Beast and the boy in the yellow star had the same eyes. Klaus bowed his head towards the war criminal, his eyes downcast, as though looking at the Butcher of Prague hurt his heart.

"Hello, Papa…" he whispered, and Vilém could feel Iveta's shock. It struck her like a bolt of electricity and she dropped the mug. The empty cup shattered beside her broken foot.

Heydrich senior didn't even look at her. He exhaled like he'd been holding his breath for weeks and fell upon his son, wrapping his arms around little Klaus. Iveta could see happy tears shining in the monster's eyes.

"Klaus, my boy!" he cried. "You've had me worried to death! What were you thinking? Are you okay? Your eye!"

Heydrich cupped his child's face in his hands, examining the boy's minor injuries. His eyes became cold. There. There was the Blonde Beast Vilém knew.

"I'll get the names of the men who did that," Heydrich vowed. "Klaus, what were you thinking, running around with this?!" He jabbed his finger at the yellow star on his child's chest. "You could have been killed!"

"That's the point!" Klaus screeched, smacking his father's hand away. Iveta felt her heart leap, but

Heydrich didn't chastise his son for the blatant disrespect. He looked down at the boy, his icy eyes melting.

"What...?" the Blonde Beast said. Klaus inhaled sharply and stepped away from his father, clutching the yellow star.

"Grandmother told me the Bible stories, the one from Exodus," the child explained clumsily. "The one with the Pharaoh and the Jews. I thought if I died like in the last plague, you'd change your heart."

"What? Klaus, you're not making any sense."

"You murdered Jan's parents!" Klaus snapped, at last lifting his eyes and meeting his father's befuddled gaze.

"Jan? Your little friend from the village? Oh, I knew we shouldn't have let you and your brother associate with Czech vermin..."

"Jan's not vermin, and he's not my friend!" Klaus cried. "He was only being nice to me because he was scared of you! Everyone's scared of you! And you sent his parents to a camp and he hates me!"

"So the Czech boy provoked this," Heydrich mumbled, standing up, a murderous shadow crossing his face. "I'll have to speak to him..."

"No, no you won't! Don't murder any more kids!" Klaus screamed. "Jan told me what you did and I didn't believe him! I thought I knew you better..."

Klaus' anger abated and sorrow took its place. His shoulders slumped and he wrapped his arms around himself, squeezing as though his favorite teddy bear was nestled against his chest. "I thought you were a hero..."

"Klaus..." Heydrich muttered, stepping towards his son, but Klaus retreated from his father's comfort.

"I looked on your desk and I saw *everything,*" Klaus cried. Iveta's gaze shifted to Heydrich. The Butcher's eyes widened for but a moment before hardening.

"Klaus, I've taught you better than this. I never should have let your grandmother fill your head with old Jew fairytales. I *certainly* never should've let you befriend undesirables. You can't understand now, but everything I do, I do so you can live in a better world one day."

"A world without Jews?" Klaus spat.

"Correct, son."

"You're a liar!" cried Klaus, "You lied to me about where the Jews go, you lied to me about the Czechs, you lied to me about everything! I don't trust you about anything anymore! You're a liar and a murderer! And I just want you to stop or else you're gonna burn in Hell forever!"

"Klaus, enough of this!" Heydrich snapped. He glanced at Iveta and Vilém could feel the girl's soul congeal as those pitiless icy eyes examined her.

"This," Heydrich declared, pointing to Iveta, "is the problem. You associate with them, you pity them, and you become weak and put yourself in danger."

"Don't hurt Iveta, she didn't do anything wrong!" Klaus snapped, grabbing his father by the belt and tugging, trying to pull his father's attention off the Jewish girl.

"She's filled your head with Jewish nonsense! She's fooled you! Klaus, I will not abide by my own son sympathizing with Jews, I'm your father and I..."

"I'd rather have a Jew for a father than you!" Klaus screeched, and the Blonde Beast's eyes erupted with anger. He raised a flat hand up, ready to slap his child across the face. Klaus seemed surprised by the concept of being struck, but only for a moment before he gritted his teeth and offered his cheek to his father.

Klaus' demonstration of bravery seemed to stir something in Heydrich. Vilém almost couldn't believe his—or, rather, Iveta's—eyes when he saw fear on the Butcher of Prague's face. The Nazi's cold eyes flitted to his own upraised hand and horror filled his features—the man could sign away a million lives, but the realization that he had even considered hitting his child horrified him. Vilém almost wanted to laugh at the absurdity.

Heydrich dropped his hand, trembling as though he had just aimed a loaded gun at his beloved boy. For a moment, there was complete silence. Iveta stared, waiting for the Butcher of Prague to decide her fate. Klaus glared at his father, tears in his eyes, and Heydrich looked from his son to his own hand, completely lost.

Finally, Heydrich let his gaze settle on his own black-gloved hand and he spoke. "We're going home, Klaus…"

"I'll run away again if you don't stop," Klaus declared. "You know I will, even if you get guards."

Heydrich chuckled. An odd sound, like a goat's bleat. "Yes…you take after me like that."

He looked down at his steely-eyed boy and commented, "Hopefully…you don't take after me in too many other ways."

"Hopefully," Klaus agreed, and Heydrich winced as though his son had buried a dagger in his heart.

"Klaus...please come home. You know I can't just quit my job. It's far too late for that."

Klaus' fists trembled and the tears he had been restraining started streaming down his face. "I know," he whimpered.

"I won't harm your friend, your little Jew friend," Heydrich said, gesturing towards Iveta. "Come home and be safe, and I'll keep her safe. As long as you're safe, she'll be safe. Deal?"

"Promise?" Klaus prodded.

"I swear to God..."

"No!" Klaus snapped, and Heydrich smirked.

"Smart boy. I swear to the Führer."

Klaus scowled and shook his head. Heydrich chuckled.

"You know me too well. I swear to you, how about that? No more lying."

Klaus looked towards Iveta. The boy wavered for a moment, as though he was tempted to resist this deal and insist that the Hangman quit, but he must have realized that he wouldn't be saving the Jews of Europe from his father anytime soon. He could, at most, save one.

"I want to be able to see her."

"Klaus..."

"I want to see her and write to her! That's the deal!"

Klaus shoved his hand towards his father, a demand for an agreement. Vilém saw a familiar smirk on Heydrich's face. That arrogant smirk he wore in the pictures Vilém saw in the exhibit, the look of a predator that had just caught a rabbit. He shook his son's hand, claiming a minor victory. The child would obey him. His little Jew friend would pay if he didn't.

Klaus yanked his hand away as soon as his father shook it, wiping his palm against his pant leg as though he had just touched dog shit. Heydrich's haughty expression shifted into sadness. He had won, but at a cost. His son would never look at him the same way again. Vilém hummed with surprise when he saw tears twinkle in the Hangman's eyes. It appeared that even for the loyal Nazi, that was a high price. Monster though he was, he seemed to love the boy.

Heydrich offered the boy his hand, this time as a father instead of a negotiator, but Klaus brushed right past him. The child ran to Iveta and hugged her.

"I'm sorry..." he whispered. Heydrich gave the little Jewish girl a venomous scowl, and all the fear, sadness, and confusion that had filled Iveta's soul boiled over and made tears attack her eyes, blinding her.

"Tell Heydrich this isn't a fucking kindergarten."

"The Reichsprotektor says..."

"Reinhard can say anything he wants, I don't care! I have enough bullshit to deal with! Just because we used to fence together doesn't mean I'm going to cover up for him!"

"I mean...he *is* your boss..."

"And I doubt *his* boss would appreciate the idea! Himmler's godson having a long-distance pet Jew...even Reinhard doesn't have enough blackmail material to get the Reichsführer to accept this!"

Vilém felt Iveta's heart tremble. She lifted her wrist to her face and wiped her tears away, clearing her vision enough for Vilém to see that the memory had shifted.

They were on familiar ground: in the Camp, in the Kommandant's office. Vilém scrutinized the Nazi, hatred burning in his soul. Raya's old boss. He saw a familiar camera sitting on the Nazi's desk, polished and pretty. Several rolls of film sat nearby, waiting for a developer.

The Nazi soldier that Klaus had been ordering around before was standing beside Iveta, fear shining in his eyes. He must have expected (and hoped) that this would be a simple drop-off mission, but Kommandant Gerber was very brave and very stupid.

The Kommandant waved his hand. "Tell you what —she can stay, but she stays with the rest of the Jews and Czechs, in the barrack..."

"General Heydrich said she is to be separated and...kept comfortable," Iveta's escort declared.

"Fucking where? All the barracks are full, my men barely have any space! What does he expect me to do, let her sleep at the foot of my bed? Give her a little collar and call her Fido?"

"Kommandant, General Heydrich asks that you consider your old friendship...and he also reminds you that you're only a Kommandant because of his generosity."

"That piece of—!" the Kommandant shouted, but he stopped himself from cursing his old "friend." He pursed his lips together, sunk down into his chair, and rubbed his forehead.

"Fine, goddamnit, I guess I'll come up with some-thing. She can be a little toy for Martin..." he mumbled. "Maybe the company will do him some good."

The Kommandant looked at the Jewish girl, peering into her eyes and making the girl's blood chill. "She looks Aryan...say, Fido, could you pretend to be German? I wouldn't want my boy to...get any ideas or become a bleeding-heart Jew-lover like Heydrich's son."

"I..." Iveta hesitated, and Vilém could feel disgust bubble up in her gut at the thought of denying her heritage. After everything she had been through because of it, to abandon it, hide it...the mere idea of doing so felt like swallowing a live slug.

"That wasn't a request, Fido. Come," the Kommandant declared, standing, strutting towards the girl, and grabbing her by one of her pigtails.

"Sir, General Heydrich said not to harm her!" Iveta's guard yelped, but the Kommandant ignored the soldier's plea and painfully yanked the girl towards the window, forcing her face against the glass.

"See that barrack over there, Barrack Four?" he sneered. Iveta barely could through the icy glass and her own tears, but she saw the wooden structure looming in the distance. She saw Nazi guards screaming and beating children with truncheons as they rushed out for roll call. She saw the young prisoners wearing rags, trembling in the cold. She saw how thin they were. She saw one little boy collapse. She saw a Nazi press a gun to the exhausted child's skull.

"That's where we put useless brats like you," the Kommandant declared as a gunshot echoed out across the Camp. Iveta whimpered, glad for her tears and the foggy glass, glad that she could barely see the boy's body.

"We sort you out from the useful workers, and little

75

drains like you get shut in there until we send you off to be put down. Get it?"

Iveta nodded, causing the Kommandant to tug on her hair. Pain shot through her scalp.

"Good Jew. The second you become useless, more trouble than you're worth, you go to Barrack Four, then you go away. To Chelmno, to Auschwitz, or maybe you end up just like that boy and you die right here. Doesn't matter to me, but for now it matters to Heydrich. You'd better be a good, quiet little Jew, and you'd better pray for Heydrich's safety. The Butcher of Prague just became your guardian angel."

The Nazi slammed the child's head against the glass, and as tears consumed Iveta's eyes, the memory shifted once more.

So I...playmate to Kommandant son. Son was good, though very quiet. Not fun like Klaus, no smiles.

"Heydrich...your guardian angel..." scoffed Vilém in disbelief.

Heydrich evil, yes, but did love Klaus. Did protect me for Klaus. Klaus wrote every week, and...I was safe...

"But...the assassination...Anthropoid..." Vilém muttered, and Iveta's vision cleared at last, revealing the new memory. A plush environment, a lavish nursery. Soft carpets, mountains of stuffed animals, a little desk, a bed with a swastika-emblazoned blanket, and so many books. Enough books to put Vilém's local library to shame. The walls were lined with ceiling-high book-shelves. The Kommandant must have truly wanted his son to be well-educated.

The boy, Little Martin, a seven-year-old with golden, carefully gelled hair, was kneeling in a corner, covering his face with his hands, counting down. "....Nine...eight....seven…"

A game of hide-and-seek. It should have been fun, but Vilém could feel that Iveta wasn't enjoying herself. She was anxious. Not playfully anxious like he remembered being when he and Erik had played hide-and-seek as children. She was waiting for something. Something bad.

She bolted out of the nursery. The Kommandant's little home was quaint, if not luxurious. Well-furnished with stolen art and Hitlerian trappings, but small. It didn't take long for Iveta to stumble across a familiar face.

"Raya…" Vilém mumbled as Iveta ducked into the developing room, shutting the door behind her. The teenage prisoner was standing by the window, massaging her burned hands.

"Fido, be careful! Don't burst in or you'll ruin the Kommandant's...pictures," Raya warned. She gestured towards a hanging line and Iveta let her eyes flit towards it for one involuntary second. The girl briefly glimpsed the images of skeletal corpses and bodies tangled in the electrified wire fence. She shivered and her eyes returned to Raya.

"He likes the ones where they're on the wire, hm? Wouldn't wanna ruin those," grumbled Iveta. "Are you okay?"

"As ever. Hide and seek?"

"Yeah."

"Little Martin won't follow you in here, he's too nice. I don't know how he and that horrible Nazi are related."

"I always say that about Klaus."

Raya's slight smile died, and Vilém knew why. Raya had been interred in the Camp during the *Heydrichiáda* —the period of repression and violent reprisals that had followed Heydrich's assassination. Iveta's so-called guardian angel was dead. Her fate was uncertain.

"Has Klaus written you?" Raya asked, and Iveta slowly shook her head.

"His father's dead."

"His father deserved worse!" hissed Raya.

"Yeah, he did, but Klaus may be sad."

"He shouldn't be…" Raya muttered.

"But he may be," Iveta sighed, fiddling with her bracelet and idly letting her eyes wander to the pictures of men tangled in the wire, her stomach roiling. No doubt she was wondering if and when a picture of her body would end up in Raya's developing room.

A noise made Iveta's heart stop. The slam of a door.

"He's back," Raya whispered. "You...you should hide…"

"No," Iveta said, squeezing her wrist, pressing the star beads on her bracelet into her skin. "Enough hiding. If he's gonna kill me, hidin' won't matter."

She smiled at Raya, offered her a hand, and the two prisoners clung to one another for a moment.

"Bye, Raya, sorry I didn't know ya' very long. Please remember me."

"I will," Raya vowed, and Vilém felt his heart crack.

Iveta marched out of the developing room, still clutching her bracelet, squeezing it so hard that the beads bore into her skin and it hurt. She accepted the pain and strutted towards the front door with her head held high.

The Kommandant was dressed in full regalia, his medals glistening on his breast as he stumbled into his home, exhausted. He took off his hat and tossed it at a hook without looking, grumbling when it fell to the floor, but evidently deciding he was too tired to give a shit about his uniform and leaving it where it was. He looked towards Iveta, initially smiling, perhaps mistaking her for his son, but when he saw her his smile became a sneer.

"Fido," he said with a nod.

"How was the funeral?"

"How was the funeral...?" The Kommandant strode towards her, annoyance shining in his eyes.

"How was the funeral, Kommandant Gerber?" Iveta growled through clenched teeth, and the Kommandant petted her head like she was a hound that had just learned to roll over.

"Good Jew. The funeral was fine, but I'm going to assume you don't care about the glitz and glamor. Heydrich got what he deserved."

Iveta barely suppressed a snort. The Kommandant scowled at her, but seemed to decide that defending his dead "friend" wasn't worth the effort.

"Buried with honors, all that. But you're just upset because your guardian's dead. Worried about going to Barrack Four, aren't you?"

Iveta looked down at her bracelet.

"Well?" the Kommandant prodded.

"I guess..." the girl answered.

"Well, you're lucky Heydrich's boy is such a pain-in-the-ass. Came up to me at his own father's funeral to threaten me if I laid a hand on you. Little shit wasn't even crying. Kinda makes me feel bad for Heydrich."

Gerber waltzed into the kitchen and poured himself a drink. Iveta followed slowly, eyeing the nearby knife rack with hesitant desire. She thought about stealing one of the blades and stabbing the wicked Nazi when his back was turned, but her gut objected, her mind summoned an image of Ilona mercy-killing their mother, and she dismised the notion. She didn't have the strength, the stomach, or the nerve for it. Besides, it wouldn't do anyone any good. They would find another monster to replace him and she would be sent to the Pit.

There were two chairs at the kitchen table, and nearby was a dirty red dog bowl labelled, "Fido." Vilém felt ill. The Kommandant had refrained from physically harming Klaus' friend, but he still insisted on dehumanizing her.

"Since Heydrich's a martyr now, Himmler and the Führer will be extra nice to his children," Gerber said, downing a shot. "So congratulations, Fido: you get to stay until the boy gets bored with you. Or until he chokes on his silver spoon, whichever comes first. Speaking of which…"

The Kommandant reached into his pocket and pulled out a balled-up envelope. "The Heydrich boy wanted me to give you this. I have a feeling it wouldn't make it past the censors. Go to your house and read it, then burn it."

She nodded, grabbing the crumpled paper and running out of the kitchen, then out the front door.

The Kommandant's "home" was, in fact, a refurbished barrack. He must have previously lived off-site and then decided to bring his home closer to work. Vilém saw a small plaque hidden beneath the white paint, partially obscured by a flowerpot. "BARRACK 1."

Iveta walked along the raised flowerbed, avoiding the carefully kept lawn and the cornflowers. Behind the former barrack, on a corner of the property full of weeds, was an old doghouse barely suitable for an animal. There was a hole in the roof, mold feeding on the wood, and sopping blankets lining the hard floor. She crawled in and carefully tore the envelope open.

It was a drawing, and Vilém could see why Klaus had felt the need to dodge the censors. The drawing was sloppy and (because the Kommandant had crumpled it up) hard to see, but Iveta could make it out. A land of fire, a smiling demon, a gate with a blazing warning: "Abandon All Hope Ye Who Enter Here."

And Reinhard Heydrich, helpfully labeled "Papa", was boiling in a cauldron full of blood while Satan stirred the pot with a pitchfork. Above the scene of Hell, Klaus had drawn a line to symbolize the divide between the underworld and earth, and above the line he had drawn himself, standing before a gravestone labeled "Papa", holding a rose, crying.

Iveta laughed, laughed and laughed until her sides ached. She fell against the wall of her doghouse and splinters stabbed her skin. She laughed even as it hurt, even as tears flooded her eyes.

"Hey…" A timid voice interrupted her cackling. She looked up and saw Little Martin kneeling in front of the doghouse. She could hardly see him through her tears.

"Found you…" the boy whimpered, and the memory shifted.

"Iveta!"

"Klaus?!"

Vilém felt a hurricane of emotions tear through Iveta's head. Joy, surprise, and relief, perhaps because she hadn't heard her true name in so long. Iveta cried with happiness as Klaus ran into the Kommandant's house and wrapped his arms around his friend, twirling her around.

"You look good!" Klaus cried, tugging on the straps of a brown box-shaped satchel that hung from his shoulders. "They've been feeding you? Taking good care of you?"

"Anything for the son of a German hero," the Kommandant mumbled. He grabbed Little Martin's hand and dragged him into the kitchen, shutting the door behind him and leaving Klaus alone with the Jewish girl.

"How's he, really?" Klaus asked, his expression becoming severe. Iveta chewed on her lip and fiddled with her bracelet.

"He's awful, but he could be worse," she sighed.

"He could be my dad," grumbled Klaus, but he shook his head, banishing his father from his brain and brightening up again. "Wanna go outside and play? Look what I brought!"

He swung his satchel off his shoulder and dropped it on the ground. Vilém was surprised the little boy had been able to lift it so easily: judging by the *thud* it made upon striking the ground, it was hefty. The satchel popped open, revealing that it was stuffed to the brim with toys. Iveta grinned, grabbed a toy dagger, and a battle began.

Iveta and Klaus took the satchel and ran outside. They spent the next hour playing with toy daggers, planes, and cars. They had a marvelous time; Iveta's soul was light as a balloon. When weariness finally forced her to rest, she sat beside Klaus on the raised flowerbed, smiling so wide her face hurt.

"I'm happy you came, I haven't seen you in so long," Iveta said. Klaus dug around his now almost-empty satchel and took out a small toy dog.

"For you!" he said. "I wanted to get you a doll, but I dunno if you like them and my little sister probably would'a stole it."

"Haha! Thanks…" mumbled Iveta, and Vilém felt a pang in her heart. Her eyes shifted towards her doghouse. Klaus had no idea, and Vilém sensed that Iveta didn't want to tell him just how bad she had it. He had already done all he could.

She set the dog next to her and rubbed her bracelet between her fingers. "Have you and your family been doing…okay?"

"Yeah," Klaus sighed. "Godfather Hein…err, Reichsführer Himmler has been very…nice…he sent us a lot of gifts. He's coming to Prague to visit soon. My little sister's really upset. Papa was always sweet to her, and she's really little and doesn't understand…"

"And you?"

Klaus laughed. "I think I understand too much. So does Mama."

A shadow fell upon Klaus' face. "I think she knew. I had trouble getting her permission to come here, had to threaten to tell everyone in my Hitler Youth battalion about the camps. Mama doesn't like me talking to Jews....ha! She ended up dragging some Jews from the Terezin Ghetto to our house. They're building us a new pool."

He grabbed his satchel and looked into it, a feeble attempt to avoid Iveta's eyes. "I don't even wanna pool."

"The Jews...?"

"They live in a shed. I keep trying to sneak them some food, but Mama catches me. Look."

He rolled up his sleeve, showing off four welts on his pale skin. Vilém didn't feel a surge of shock fill Iveta's mind upon seeing the injuries, and he could only assume that was because of the era. Corporal punishment must have been relatively universal.

"Gotta get used to it," Klaus sighed. "Since Papa's gone."

"He didn't hit you?" Iveta queried, raising an eyebrow.

"Never, and he never let Mama hit us either, no matter what we did. Believe it or not, Papa was the one who let us get away with everything. Mama's the strict one. I remember one time...we were all in Berlin at this party thing for all the important people in the Reich and my brother and I got into the fireworks. I ended up settin' em off...what a mess! Almost killed the Führer...almost killed my dad too...and Mama wanted to thrash my ass...but Papa just laughed it off..."

Before Klaus could say another word, he spotted

something at the bottom of his satchel. Slowly, the boy pulled out a white teddy bear.

"Heldi...?" Iveta queried. Klaus didn't answer. He let the satchel slip from his grasp and held the teddy bear close to his face, staring into its black button eyes.

"I should have..." he whispered. "I wish I'd killed 'em back then...everything would be fine if he died back then!"

He stood up and threw the bear. The stuffed animal landed in the mud beside Iveta's doghouse. Iveta looked up at the boy, fear flowing through her veins. His face was twisted in anger, his eyes flaring. Klaus Heydrich looked too much like his father right then.

But the moment was short lived, and although the boy still looked angry, tears fell from his eyes and he regained his innocence. He plopped back down, wrapping his arms around himself.

Iveta recognized what he needed right away. Without hesitation, she threw her arms around the boy. She felt Klaus resist instinctively for a moment—perhaps a small part of him was still trained to fear a Jew's touch, or perhaps he thought he didn't deserve her affection. Either way, he stiffened for only a moment before sinking into the hug.

"I cried when he died..." the boy confessed. "Is...is that okay?"

"Yes, Klaus, that's okay," Iveta assured him, hugging him tighter.

"I miss him...is that okay?"

"I think that's okay, Klaus..." Iveta released him, keeping one hand on his shoulder and making sure he looked into her eyes as she smiled at him. She stood, ran to where the bear had fallen, and picked it up.

A shudder went up her spine. Reinhard Heydrich had bought that bear with money he earned by slaughtering her people. Heydrich and his murderous hands had touched that bear. It almost felt cursed, but she ignored the squeamish sensation that filled her as she held the toy and carried it back to Klaus. The boy hugged Heldi close to his heart, wiping his tears on the bear's head.

"I wanna go ice skating," Klaus whimpered. "Or ride my bike....but it's not fair if I do that while you're in here, it's not fair."

"It's not fair," Iveta agreed. "But I don't want you to be miserable, Klaus. You're nice and...you tried your best."

Klaus sniffed, wiped his face on his sleeve, and smiled up at his Jewish friend. "You're the nice one. He was really wrong about you people."

"We're just people."

"Exactly..." Klaus sighed. The memory shifted, but not by much. Klaus' visit was almost at its end. He stood by a black car. Iveta approached to say goodbye, hugging the toy dog he had given her.

"Bye, Iva," Klaus said, wrapping his arms around her neck. He made sure his lips were close to her ear, casting a nervous eye towards his guard.

"Listen to me," he whispered. "I looked at more of my papa's notes, and I peeked at some of Himmler's. The other camps are so, so much worse. They do horrid things to children, especially twins and Jews that look too Aryan. Whatever you do, don't let them take you to any other camp, especially not Auschwitz. Okay? Whatever you do, don't let them take you there."

"Okay," she squeaked, and Vilém felt anxiety swarm her heart. "Goodbye, Klaus. Go have fun, please. Have fun for me."

"Promise," he vowed. He stepped back, glanced at the Kommandant, and suddenly leaned forward and gave Iveta a small kiss on the cheek.

"Sorry, just wanna break some laws. You know kissing Jews is illegal," he said, his eyes glistening with mischief, and Vilém could feel Iveta's cheeks heat up.

"You're horrible," she giggled.

"It's in my blood. Bye, bye, Iveta! Please stay safe!"

He climbed into the car, smirking at his guard, who gave the children a look of disgust as he slammed the door behind the Aryan boy. Iveta watched as Klaus' car zoomed away. Once it disappeared, she looked down at the toy dog. She smiled, took off her star bracelet, and put it around her new stuffed animal's neck, giving it a star-studded collar. She sighed sorrowfully, stroking the stuffed animal's head. A single reminder of her two best friends.

Iveta's ghost interjected somberly: *Klaus died three days after.*

"What?!" Vilém exclaimed.

Riding bike. Was hit by bus...I...hope he was...having fun. Hope he...was happy.

"He...that's...he didn't deserve that."

No.

"He was just a kid....he seemed nice...not his fault his dad was a shithead..."

Nobody's fault but the Nazis, yes.

"And...once he was gone..."

Kommandant decided he did not need pet Jew.

"And that's how you got here."

Yes.

"If...you don't mind me asking...how did you die?"

Months later, rumor...Barrack Four was...to Auschwitz...to go to

Auschwitz. Trains come to take us to Auschwitz. Klaus warn me. I...have good memory. Did not want to see Auschwitz.

"Oh, Iveta..." Vilém said. The memory shifted. It was so dark that Vilém could barely make out what was going on, but he felt the girl roll off her wooden bunk and crawl to the middle of the barrack. She carried the stuffed dog under her arm: either the Kommandant had let her keep it or she had been clever enough to smuggle it with her into Barrack Four. Either way, she pried a loose floorboard upwards. The star bracelet around the dog's neck shimmered slightly in what little light the barrack allowed in. Iveta kissed the gift from her sister.

"Bye, Ilona..." she whispered, shoving the bracelet-clad toy beneath the floorboards. "Sorry I wasn't brave enough."

She stood, took a deep breath, and everything that happened next happened so quickly that Vilém barely felt a thing: Iveta sprinted towards the door and her tiny body broke the flimsy lock. Guards shouted, dogs barked, a shot was fired.

She ran for the electrified fence, leapt upon it. There was pain only for a moment, the smell of burned skin, and then everything went dark.

Vilém opened his eyes and once more he found

himself in Barrack Four. He could feel the little hairs on his arms and legs standing erect, as though an electric current had really gone through his body. He took a moment to breathe deeply and let his soul recover from experiencing death again before he reached out and touched the glass display.

"So...Iveta...thank you for showing me what happened to you. It must have been hard. You're a brave girl."

Danke...

"I really wanna help you, help you move on. What can I do to help you finish your business on earth?"

Iveta answered, and Vilém felt his heartbeat stall.

"Oh..." he sighed, smiling. "That'll get me fired. Let's do it."

Sladký's Sweets rarely had an early customer. Occasionally, some children would pop in on their way to school or a husband would run in desperate for a last-minute anniversary gift, but most of their clientele didn't arrive until the afternoon. Jana usually spent the morning making candies and restocking the shelves.

She was surprised, then, when she emerged from the stockroom lugging a box full of taffy and saw a young man leaning against the display case. She smiled at him, concern filling her heart when she saw the bags under his eyes. It looked like he hadn't slept for a week.

"You're not getting anything for free, Vilém," she

teased. Before Vilém could even think of retorting, his stomach did so for him, snarling like a starved bear.

"No breakfast?" Jana guessed, and Vilém nodded. She plopped the box of taffy down by a table laden with jars and started refilling the glass containers. "Oh, all right: take a brownie. Not nutritious, but it'll tide you over!"

"You're an angel!" Vilém chuckled, swiping a brownie and devouring it in two bites. With his stomach somewhat sated, he marched towards Jana and grabbed a handful of watermelon-flavored taffy, shoving it into the appropriate jar.

"Thanks! I hate restocking, especially the taffy," Jana said.

"No problem. Hey, Jana, remember how you said your grandma could kick my ass?"

"Yup! You wanna challenge her? She's upstairs," Jana said, pointing towards the roof. "She lives right above the shop."

"I actually wanted to talk to her. I think I found something...someone, actually. Your grandma survived the war?"

"No, she died," snickered Jana, and Vilém grabbed the now empty box and bopped her on the shoulder.

"I'm being serious, Jana," he said, though he couldn't suppress a smile. "While I was at the Camp the other day, I...well, I think I found something your grandmother would really appreciate. Your grandma's name's Ilona, right?"

"Yup!"

"And she was born in the Sudetenland?"

"Jesus...you really did your homework."

"I had some inside help."

"Y'know, most girls would find this a little creepy," Jana said, offering him a bottle of hand sanitizer.

"Trust me, I was just as surprised as you are. More, actually. Just really good timing, I guess. It's actually about her twin sister…"

Jana slammed her hand on the pump, sending a stream of sanitizer into her palm. She cursed and Vilém grabbed some napkins, helping her clean up the mess of gel.

"Sorry…I didn't know my grandma had a twin…" mumbled Jana, wrinkling her nose as the store's pervasive scent of sugar was overpowered by the odor of alcohol. "She, uh…she doesn't like talking about the war. I'm warning you, you might get your ass kicked."

"I'll survive," Vilém said. "Is it okay if I go up and talk to her?"

"Yeah, please…and when you're done, if you're still alive, I wanna hear everything," Jana said, a glimmer in her eyes. She looked at him with appreciation, as though the little grain of information about her family was a precious treasure he had gifted her. He almost wanted to kiss her right then, but he held back, instead running to the staircase and blowing her a kiss.

"It's a long story, I'll tell you over dinner!" he declared, and Jana laughed. A musical sound. He would need to make her laugh more often.

Vilém darted up to the second story and after knocking on a few doors, an aged voice called out, "Jana, sweet-love, what in God's name are you doing out there?"

"Ms. Sladký?" Vilém cried. "I'm a friend of Jana's, my name's Vilém…"

"Oh, come in, you asshole! I was wondering when I'd get a chance to put you through the wringer!"

Vilém chuckled and entered. Ilona Sladký sat in a wheelchair, watching as two little zebra finches flitted about in a cage by the window, tousling over twine. She looked good for her age: her blonde pigtails had been replaced with a gray bun, and her blue eyes burned with a fire only slightly less intense than the inferno they had held as a child. Merely from her appearance, Vilém could tell Jana had been right—she could kick his ass.

"Sit, sit!" she cried, waving towards a red couch. He obeyed and sat across from her. A black Chihuahua snarled at him from the floor, but remembered its training and didn't lunge for his ankles.

"Bayaya doesn't like you, that's bad news!" Ilona cried. "Jana seems to, though. Won't shut up about you, ha! Bless that girl, but she has such a terrible taste in men. I hope you're not another mistake."

"I hope so too. Has she really been talking about me that much?"

"Non-stop! She was so upset when you wouldn't answer her texts! I was about to hunt you down, but then when you called her back, she was bouncing off the walls! I've never seen her so excited! She said you were gorgeous."

"Your verdict?" Vilém queried, and Ilona roared with laughter.

"Oh, I like you! So what brings you into the lion's den this early?"

"It actually doesn't have anything to do with Jana,"

Vilém said, reaching into his pocket. "Has Jana told you I work at the Camp a few miles outside town? I'm the night security."

"Ah…" Ilona's entire body stiffened, and Bayaya seemed to sense his master's discomfort. The tiny dog leapt into the old woman's lap and started licking her shaking, liver-stained hands.

"I hope this isn't another attempt at…at getting me to give a testimonial for some little exhibit…I'm not interested. I'd like to die without being pitied, I don't want to be an artifact…"

"Far from it, Ilona…."

"Ha! Are we on a first name basis, son?"

"No, sorry, it's just a force of habit. By any chance, Ms. Sladký, do you believe in ghosts?"

"I don't believe in anything I can't see with my own two eyes, and even then, I try to be skeptical."

"I don't blame you, and I know this will sound crazy, but…for the last couple of nights, I've been speaking with your sister, Iveta."

The old woman's eyes widened and she hugged her dog so tightly it yipped and fought back, tumbling off her lap and retreating under the couch. Vilém hoped he hadn't given the old woman a heart attack: Ilona must have known right then that something was amiss. If even her granddaughter didn't know about Iveta, Jana's new boyfriend shouldn't have had the slightest clue.

"Have you people been…digging into my family? There's no way you could know about her unless you started looking into…documents or birth records…"

"I'm not a historian, Ms. Sladký. Wouldn't know the

first thing about archives. I only know what I've been told."

"And...what have you been told?" whispered Ilona, forcing her eyes off the man, staring at the finches and tightening her jaw. One of the birds had won the battle. The victor nibbled on the thread while the loser sat at the bottom of the cage, despondent.

"I know you two were twins. On your birthday, she tried to make you a cake and burned it, and you made her a bracelet with star beads. I know you two loved astronomy. She wanted to go to college, you just wanted to stay close to her. You two used to play together in an old watchtower you guys called the Star Shack..."

Every unknowable fact made Ilona's eyes bulge wider and wider. Her slight trembling became quaking.

"You can't know all this..." she whispered, keeping her gaze locked onto the cage, on the defeated finch.

"Are you okay? Should I...?"

"I've survived worse than the truth!" Ilona snapped, finally facing him again. Tears shimmered in her eyes.

"I know you did what you had to for your mother," Vilém said gently. "You don't have anything to be afraid of, Ilona. I'm not here to judge you."

Ilona covered her mouth with her hands, muffling a sob. Her mother. She must have forced herself to forget that day.

"God almighty, Iveta's at the Camp...?" whimpered Ilona. "She's still here..."

"She's been here for decades."

"Why? W-what happened to her?! Did she say what happened to her?!"

"Yes...you, uh...you know the boy, Klaus, you know he was Reinhard Heydrich's son..."

"I know...I found out after the war..." Ilona whispered, rolling the word "war" on her tongue. She must have spent a lifetime avoiding that word. It must have felt so strange to utter it at last. "He was the reason I never went back to our village and burned it to the ground. By the time it was all over and I gave up looking for Iva, all the monsters who...hurt us...and our mother...they were dead. Only their children remained, and if Iveta could love the Blonde Beast's son...what else could I do but...nothing? Let it all go...like a coward..."

"You're not a coward, Ilona," Vilém assured her, repressing a smile. It seemed Klaus had saved some lives after all. If he bumped into the boy's ghost, he would have to tell him that.

"Don't tell me I'm brave for surviving, surviving doesn't take bravery! Iveta was ten times braver than me!" hissed Ilona, digging her nails into the armrest of her wheelchair.

"She was brave, very brave right until the end," Vilém said. He told Ilona everything that had happened to Iveta after they were separated. Ilona listened, glowering down at Bayaya's toys as Vilém told her about Iveta's status as a pet Jew.

"I knew she died at the Camp. I found one of the pictures the Kommandant took of her...her on the wire...I didn't know she lived with the Kommandant...a doghouse..." Ilona shook her head, looked into Vilém's eyes with morose tenderness and said, "Thank you, young man...for telling me this, but...I don't understand why she didn't speak to me the last time I was at the Camp. After the war, I went there, I found out she had died there…"

"And then you never went back," Vilém said. "You settled here, lived your life, and you've felt guilty about it every day. Every day, you think you should have been the one to break down those stairs. Iveta read you like a book, Ilona. She knows what you're feeling."

Ilona pulled her headscarf over her mouth and nose, sobbing into the soft fabric. "I should have been the one to jump!" she cried. "I was a coward, and then I gave up and did nothing!"

"You lived. You married. You had children. You started a business. You did everything she wanted you to, Ilona…" Vilém stood, walked to the old woman, and knelt before her, putting a hand on her wrist. "She just wants you to see that. She doesn't want you to run from the past, and she doesn't want you to be miserable. She wants you to go to the Camp and smile for her. She says she's missed your smile so much…she doesn't want to go to Heaven until she sees it again."

Vilém pulled out the treasure he had hidden in his pocket: a toy dog, still wearing the bracelet. Its time beneath Barrack Four had been harsh: holes marred its soft body, dirt had turned it brown, but still it held itself together. The star bracelet, carefully cleaned by Vilém, shimmered at Ilona.

He set the dog in her lap. For a moment, he was afraid she would toss it away, but her shaking hands reached out, lifted the little toy to her heart, and she hugged it with all the gusto of a little girl.

"*Rehor, you have some explaining to do!*"

"Ow, ow, ow!" Vilém cried. He had stepped into Barrack Four and was immediately assaulted by his boss. Ms. Doubek grabbed him by the collar and dragged him towards the Heydrich Exhibit.

"WHAT IS THIS?!" Doubek screamed, pointing to Vilém's handiwork: the display case where Klaus Heydrich's wanted poster had been resting was knocked over, the floorboard of the barrack partially torn up.

"You not only almost destroyed a historical artifact!" Doubek screamed, gesturing towards the poster. Klaus smiled weakly up at them, and Vilém could practically sense the boy's spirit apologizing for all the ruckus on his behalf.

"But you damaged the Camp's foundation! You're fired and you'll be lucky if I don't get you arrested for damaging protected historical—!"

"Oh, pipe down, you!"

Ilona's voice came, so sharp that it shut up Ms. Doubek (no small feat.) Jana helped her grandmother into the barrack, nervousness oozing from her every pore. Vilém felt too sorry for his almost-girlfriend: her first visit to a concentration camp and she had to deal with all this craziness!

Jana walked her grandmother to the upturned display case. "Here, Grandma?" she asked. Ilona nodded and Jana sunk to her knees, letting her grandmother sit on the floor.

"Ma'am, please don't sit on the..." Ms. Doubek

started to say, but Ilona gave her a withering glare and the museum director clammed up.

"Oh, quiet! My sister died here, I'll sit where I want! And this young man found a valuable and meaningful *artifact*!" She spat the word as though it were a curse, pulling the bracelet-clad toy dog from her pocket and placing it in front of the broken floorboard.

"If you fire him, you'll be firing a kind soul who helps Holocaust survivors!" Ilona decreed. "Vilém, don't you worry about that witch! Come, sit next to me!"

Vilém, whose collar was still firmly in Ms. Doubek's grasp, shot a pleading gaze at his boss. The last thing anyone needed was two septuagenarians going to war in the middle of the Camp. Ms. Doubek scowled at her employee and released him.

"You're lucky," she said, pointing towards Ilona. "I like her more than I like Heydrich's kids."

She marched out of the barrack, muttering about phone calls and lawsuits, leaving Vilém and the Sladkýs to themselves.

"This is so crazy…" Jana whispered.

"You always pick the crazies," Ilona said, pinching her granddaughter's cheek. Jana snickered.

"I wouldn't have believed you, Vil, but my grandma never trusts anyone and you somehow convinced her to come here," Jana said. "That's enough for me."

Vilém blushed, but before he could say a word, Ilona snapped her fingers right in front of his nose. "No flirting right now! Iveta first!"

"Okay…everyone put your hand on the dog and close your eyes…" Vilém instructed. In sync, the three reached out and touched the fake fur, shutting their eyes.

"Iveta?" Vilém cried. "I brought her here."

Danke, Vilém!

"Oh my God...Iva..." whimpered Ilona. Jana bit her bottom lip. She hadn't heard a thing, but she decided not to say anything. Whatever was happening, her grandma's voice was cracking. With happiness, with sorrow, with everything.

Hi, sis, Iveta said, switching to her native German and cutting Vilém out of their conversation.

"I...Iveta...I'm so sorry..." Ilona sobbed.

You don't have to be sorry, sis!

"But you're in here and I...I..."

That's your granddaughter?! She's so pretty! I hope she and Vilém stay together. He's been so nice, listening to me even when he didn't want to. He's a wonderful man. He told you everything?

"Yes...I can't believe you had to go through that. Iva, why did you jump that day?"

For you! To be brave like you. I love you and you always protected me. I just wanted to make sure you could live and...you did! But I thought you would come to the Camp and maybe bring your family. You never did.

"I'm sorry, Iva..." sobbed Ilona. "You were the brave one after all. I was too scared and guilty to come here, to remember how...unfair everything was. I didn't even tell my children about you. I felt like...if I avoided you, didn't talk about you or any of it...maybe the brick on my heart would go away. It's so unfair! I got my sweet shop like I always wanted and a nice wedding and beautiful children...and you never got to study the stars."

I'll see them up close very soon. But I wanted to see you and make sure you were happy. You are happy, right? Please be happy for me, not despite me. I want you to come here all the time and remember me, then go out and laugh and eat lots of candy. I want you to come here and smile for me, okay?

"Yes…I'll smile for you, Iva…"

I love you, sis. I'll kiss Mama for you. Goodbye.

And with that, Vilém and Ilona felt Iveta's presence dissipate as she pranced into the unknown.

"What happened? What'd she say?" Jana asked. She opened her eyes and looked at her companions. Vilém wore a somewhat befuddled expression of contentment.

And Ilona…Jana felt her heart flutter. The most beautiful smile in existence bloomed upon the face of Ilona Sladký.

AFTERWORD

Thank you for reading Barrack Four!
The sequel, Barrack Three, will be available on
November 28th, 2020!
If you would like to read more stories like this one,
follow Project 613 on Twitter @Project613Books, on
Facebook, and sign up for updates at Project613Publish-
ing.com!